when the dust

finally

settles

Kat Meads

Also by Kat Meads:

Essays: *Born Southern and Restless*
Fiction: *The Invented Life of Kitty Duncan*
          Little Pockets of Alarm
          Not Waving
          Sleep
          Stress in America
          Wayward Women
Poetry: *Filming the Everyday*
          Night Bones
          The Queendom
          Quizzing the Dead

Cover image: "Farm Painting" by Philip Rosenthal; by permission

Copyright © 2011 by Kat Meads
Published by Ravenna Press
Spokane, Washington, USA
www.ravennapress.com

ISBN: 978-0-9835982-1-3
LCCN: 2011906578

FIRST EDITION

For my brother, Craig
with me
in the long gone/back when

when the dust

finally

settles

Clarence Carter

You think the dead don't hear and see—backwards, forwards, all at once, piecemeal, big picture, best and worst?

Surprises coming your way, my friend, that much I guarantee.

You go by the majority, fearing death turns out to be a big chunk of what living is, people more or less sniffing the stench of end before dropping a molar, fretting in advance about the where, when, how soon, how hard, who'll care, who won't. Another example, if you're looking, how Clarence Carter skirted the average, plowed his own row so to speak, disinclined to anguish over either side of the great divide. A gift for the carefree, you might call it, though folks in Mawatuck did and do tag it something different.

No need to be a spook to hear this particular deceased passed judgment on, ridiculed in best Christian fashion. Go ahead. Nose around, groundside. Take one of those house-to-house opinion polls. Won't get a single door slammed in your face, probably get invited in for sugar tea and cake while my former neighbors confide the long and shortcomings of Clarence Carter.

Favorite Mawatuck sport, Clarence Carter gossip.

That'd be my doing, mostly.

"Clarence? Certainly I knew Clarence Carter. Craziest man, white or black, county-wide."

"Big man. Crazy and big. What you asking about Clarence for?"

"Blessed land! The man was lazy. Triflin'. Wouldn't lift a finger. Wouldn't work to save his soul."

"Let his family farm go to ruin. Didn't have far to go, but it was Clarence let it bottom out. Had no interest in farming. Least none that showed."

"What you curious about Clarence for?"

Friendliness cooling a bit. Eyes starting to cut, bottoms starting to fidget. Own slices of sweet starting to languish on the plate.

How come?

Because that Mawatuck rule of treating strangers kindly, even snooping ones, just ran hard up against the suspicion that you, stranger, must be a mite touched yourself to come around begging to confirm the obvious: that Clarence Carter was a man lacked common sense and every other grade besides.

Don't matter. Ole Clarence is privy to all kinds of secrets, confidences and pitiless facts those neighbors of mine don't know and never will.

First off: I wasn't a day in life crazy. *Pretended* to be afflicted. Convinced every sharp and dull-witted local I was, government boys too. And regardless what my Rosie claims, this ignorant swamp Cracker would have kept on conning them government boys if the Oliver hadn't reared up like a startled crane, flipping itself and me one windless afternoon, temperature hot as midsummer. Here's why: because every day I breathed I got a little better at gauging how much or little set Mawatuck talking and delivering up oddities in just that amount. Tell you another thing: when Clarence Carter was alive, no Mawatuck citizen ever finished a hard day's labor without thanking Jesus for not being him or his nearest blood kin. Performed a valuable community service, I did, giving every man, woman and child chance to knuckle-point and pity, feel superior, no matter how bad off that superior was.

Folks miss that kind of comfort. Sure they do.

Where I went wrong—you paying attention? 'Cause here's another something I kept tight to my chest till it cracked open like a walnut hull—where I made my mistake was thinking I could set gossips talking, then cut off that tattle when I had a mind to. Turns out tattle reseeds itself same as weed, only faster. Turns out starting and stopping a story ain't part of the same feed barrel.

So enjoy those Clarence Carter tales you'll hear, door-to-door visiting. They're plenty entertaining, if I do say so myself. But if you're seeking God's truth and nothing spicier believe only up to the part where the tractor did a cartwheel, punctured my rib bones, gouged my heart. Rest is nonsense, work of imagination darker than mine. Accident finished me off, nothing more peculiar or calculated than that. Didn't want to die, didn't plan on dying that afternoon, but when I understood the end was fast coming, realized where that airborne machine would squarely land, so help me, I did, I giggled—a giggle sane as any shriek because once in this world you're already on the road to leaving it, so why not go out giggling?

If a giggle's what you're after yourself, suggest to the pious folks of Mawatuck crazy Clarence made his exit laughing.

Lord a-mercy, as my Rosie would say.

They'd quicker believe I was the devil's daughter than accept such rank sacrilege. No trouble calling me a sinful disgrace, of no count to bush or beast, but met my Maker grinning?

"Naw, naw. I cain't sanction that kind of talk."

"Naw, naw. You won't get me to believe that—not even of Clarence Carter."

Which might set YOU to thinking *uh-huh, uh-huh, so why trust a man dead as dirt?*

Best give a spook some leeway, see what happens there. Because another nugget of pure truth? Just because you can't trust a man alive don't mean you shouldn't trust that same son of a bitch dead. Lot of misunderstandings get cleared up, lot of puzzles get solved, once you can't do a thing but watch and listen and wish you'd done better by loved ones.

Wishing is what keeps the dead dying.

Best prepare yourself for that too.

Harrison Doxey

White girls.

The shit they talk.

Haven't shut up, not once, entire wait in this tricked out gym. Allison Ferrell and her lapdog Melinda Larson. SO excited over some latticework screen. The very sight flipping them into prom night memoryland.

Ooo, oooo!

"It IS the same, the very same," says Allison, going dreamy like white girls do, half her brain living in fantasy land, allowed to.

"It IS," Melinda repeats, same dreamy voice, same eyelash flutter, because if Allison dove headfirst into a pond of piss, Melinda would jump right in behind her. Which works out fine because Allison won't fart without her Melinda audience.

Bad enough waiting to practice palming a diploma, worse to be bunched in a gym's lobby listening to white girl yap. But how else you going to pass the time except sit, sweat and try to go deaf?

Mawatuck Class of '68, all 48 of us, supposed to be lined up nice and tidy, short to tall. Standing straight up, at attention, ready to strut-march to a folding chair. Nobody leaning, nobody squatting, nobody's ass to the ground.

Uh-huh.

Been waiting two hours already for that scheduled skip-along, no sign of it happening in another two. Mrs. Broome screaming like a red-haired maniac. Florist shoving the same two potted palms back and forth across a lopsided stage. Mrs. Avery clutching a clipboard, looking for all the world like a put-upon darkie in captivity. Every one of those folded chairs still folded, piled offside. Bleachers roped off for a chorus yet to arrive. But that hardly matters since the organ's missing too. "Where's the organ? They promised they'd deliver the organ by eight!" The Broomstick's been fuming over that slipup ever since she took charge of this Saturday gym.

Bleachers, rafters, nobody can do fuck-all to decorate those, but the commencement crew wants that basketball hoop *covered*, man. Lackey after lackey has skittered up ladders, lugging canvas.

Draping a backboard—shit.

Exactly what it looks like: shit.

The Broomstick must think the same, the way she's shrieking, face red as her wig hair.

Cement's cooler than air, but pretty soon this lobby's going to heat up like the inside of my Firebird. How much shade can a low hedge provide? Next to none. Lucian parked his Fairlaine same stretch of green, close as he could without risking a scratch. Brand new, every bolt and gasket on my Firebird, but Lucian's just as foolish about protecting his Fairlaine. Rebuilt that car chassis to roof, fenders, brake line, windshield, all replaced, then repainted it godawful turquoise.

"What kind of nigger color is that?" Jimmy Barnard asked, me standing right there.

"White-nigger blue," Lucian said. "You got a problem with my choice of white-nigger blue?"

Which made Jimmy snigger through his nose. The end. Guys runty as Jimmy Barnard can't afford to have a problem with guys Lucian-size.

Too bad bigness or *something* won't shut Allison Ferrell's mouth.

"Nell? Did you notice? The latticework screen behind the stage?"

Uh-oh.

Major meanness gearing up. You can always tell with Allison. Cocks her head, pinches her ear, fiddles with her earrings. And Nell Stallings, you'd swear she wasn't pure white herself, the way Allison plays her. It's like somebody forgot to slip Nell her copy of the Pale Girl's Guidebook. That, or she skimmed what she should have underlined.

"Over in the corner, don't you remember? The photographer had everybody pose in front of it for prom pictures?"

Allison's twitching that pointing finger same way she twitches her butt.

"Nell!"

"What?"

"Do you—or don't you—remember?"

"Remember what?"

"That latticework screen at the prom?"

"Hard to remember what you weren't there to see."

Pretty good comeback—except that's exactly what Allison wanted Nell to confess.

"Oh THAT'S right. You couldn't come."

"WOULDN'T come."

"Wouldn't because no one asked."

Allison tee-hees, Melinda tee-hees.

White girls.

"Remember the theme, Melinda?" Allison's dreamy voice again. "'Sweet Surrender.' Remember 'Sweet Surrender'?"

What's dumber? Decorating a gym for commencement or decorating it "Sweet Surrender"? Crepe paper streamers, plastic roses, pink paper hearts. Asked my date from Central if she wanted one of those hearts, ready to snatch and run. But she passed. Didn't *get* it. The whole joke of going to whitey's prom. The dig of driving up in a washed and waxed Firebird, prancing real color into that pink and pastel crowd, dancing to their dinky do-wah band. If Jocelyn McPherson had deigned to show, we could have shared a low-down gut laugh at that dance floor spectacle. Arms flapping, legs jerking, looking more like they were dodging knives than grooving. Mini-lesson in spaz, whites dancing. Can't get loose, can't let go. Always fighting for control. And all the while thinking *white be cool, white be cool.*

Nell Stallings in an evening dress.

Huh.

That might be a sight more pitiful than dance spaz. Collarbones exposed, sticking out sharp over netting. Not too fetching, that picture. The girl's seriously bulk-deprived.

Seriously and then some.

"Hey, Broomstick! This show ever gonna start?"

A teacher, even on the other side of the gym, still has teacher ears. Soon as she picks up that Broomstick jive, she swings round, starts barreling in our direction, squalling orders, whole trip.

"When I said LINE, I meant LINE."

Thing is, no one much cares what she meant or means. She's a teacher, but a teacher losing hold. Week or so from now we can all spit into that plot of hairspray and howling will be the Broomstick's one and only revenge.

"Why can't we practice *barefoot*?"

Reasonable question.

Not my whine, my reasonable.

Practicing in graduation shoes only stinks up your hoofers in advance.

But the Broomstick's not chummy with reasonable.

Cramps her style.

"One more smart remark—from anyone—and none of you comes near a diploma. Understand?"

Here's what we understand: this wait we're all stuck in? Us and the Broomstick? Nowhere near finished. Nowhere near coming to its end.

But there's one pair of feet sweating where the Broomstick wants them. Nell Stallings's dress-up pumps, heels about half as high as Allison's, might have started out white and new but they're dinged and smudgy now.

For a shrimpy girl, Nell Stallings walks on substantial feet. Real clodhoppers, man.

She's gazing back where Lucian's testing card tricks on Jimmy Barnard. Gazing and clapping her knees together, shooting out her lip every now and again to breath-blow hair out of her eyes. Doesn't call out, but all the same Lucian looks up like he's been radared.

To protect "Amelia Nell," Lucian might even let his crazy daddy go wanting. Blood-related somehow. Not close cousins but could be the way they shove and jaw, like they've known each other forever and don't expect that knowing to change.

Like that.

Ambling over, Lucian brings his cigarette too.

Teachers.

What they don't hear, they smell.

"Is that a *cigarette*, Lucian Carter?"

Jimmy Barnard doubles over, screech-laughing because, this close to graduation, against all party instincts, it *is* plain old tobacco Lucian's sucking on.

"NO smoking in the gym."

"Graduate's privilege," Lucian says.

"NO SMOKING IN THE GYM, I SAID!"

Like louder will carry the day. The usual Broomstick strategy.

"GRADUATE'S PRIVILEGE!"—even louder, because Lucian's having too much fun to give it up.

"You haven't graduated YET, little man."

"Did she actually say LITTLE?!?!"

Off stride today, no question.

"Outside! Now!"

On the go-by, Lucian gives me a wink, ignoring the "bye, Lucian, bye," coming from moony June-y Melinda, wearing love like a wart, looking so pathetic Nell and Allison share a one-time same moment/same object smirk.

But Lucian, man, he's already gone, back out into the fry-heat of the day. Outside with the rest of the white boys, all of them, even the field-bred, thinking sun's such a pleasure. Welcome to it. Welcome to those glare rays. This butt stays parked shade-side.

Look out.

Plastic rolling.

Got to take precautions against spike heels the likes of Allison's. Can't have a playing court full of divots, can't allow that kind of interference. Might cost Mawatuck Hornets a game. Can't risk that for nothing, man.

Mawatuck *Rebels* used to be before the school board had to, fast, think up something less *Old* South. Playing for the Mawatuck Hornets, even black boys get cheered—long as we're scoring goals, winning games. Long as. But when the booing starts, who gets the most flak?

Uh-huh.

Federal government could have ordered integration, sent in the Army *and* the Marines and county whites would still have resisted tooth and nail. But spin it as a chance to win tournaments and here come platoons of jowly white men, falling all over themselves, simpering, begging.

Throw over that all-black school, son.

Plenty of seats on OUR bus.

Plenty of chairs in the lunchroom.

I'm telling you, Wilbur, these boys CAN PLAY BALL. We get them enrolled before next basketball season, we'll wallop Creswell. Conference title, tournament championship, district honors. Hell, maybe even STATE.

Bad case of trophy hunger—that's what it really took to desegregate Mawatuck High School.

Took another four years to blacken up commencement, but it's happened now. Sunday night next, the Reverend Clevon Dunston, skin the color of highway asphalt, cordially invited to sit beneath drooping canvas, wait his turn to inspire the Class of '68.

Equal opportunity snubbing, man.

Nobody listens to baccalaureate preachers, white, black, space monkey green. Other things on the brain. Gathered to graduate, not pray. He'll sneak in a prayer, though. Preachers always do. Yawns, snores, gum popping—nothing halts a preacher in prayer mode.

Our hea-ven-ly Fa-tha, we come to YOU tonight, asking that YOU, Almighty God, be with these young people as they...

Heard it all already, everything he'll blab.

Know it by heart, letter for letter, pause for pause.

...for we ask all in the name of our Lord and Savior, Jesus Christ. Amen.

Then...?

Maybe a sprinkle of a-men echoes. Maybe some call and response starting up in the black-heavy section of bleachers.

"Amen."

"Amen."

"Amen, brother."

Then...?

Those dignitaries bunched up alongside the Reverend, looking like they just swallowed dill pickles whole, forced to brother up as well.

Nah.

Never happen.

Valedictorian's got less chance than a preacher of being listened to but Jenny Lucas is practicing hard regardless. Up there on that sloping stage, clutching podium, performing her send-off speech time and again, the Broomstick making her repeat every sentence twice, top volume.

The future, *the future*, THE FUTURE!!!

Straight-A Jenny in straight-A hell.

Nell's so bored she's picked up *The Hornet's Nest*, paging through prom night highlights and, uh-oh, senior class predictions.

Surprise, surprise: Allison sticks her big nose in.

"Look! Someone thinks I'll be a Hollywood star in two years. That, or a millionaire's bride."

Uh-huh.

Someone named Melinda.

Lucian gets "Soon to be mechanic for Richard Petty." Me: "Youngest NBA Player of the Year."

"Where's your prediction, Nell?"

Like Allison doesn't know full well where it is and what that insult says. Only one surprised is the silent reader.

"'Nell Stallings: Not a clue.'"

The way Nell's curling her lip means she's decided to laugh. Edges of her mouth turn up—she gets that far before Allison blurts: "WOW! At least someone thinks I've GOT a future! At least my future's not a big fat Zeeee-ROW!"

"And on our shoulders, yours and mine," Jenny Lucas squalls, "rest the responsibility for a better tomorrow!"

Tighter and tighter Nell balls that flat page, like accusation will lose its sting crumpled.

Organ arrives. Two musclemen hauling it in. Mr. Granger, music director, creeping toward the music stand. Moving at his usual speed, in his usual crimp, like he's just been sucker-punched.

White girls, black girls, preparing to harmonize.

Black sopranos get applauded same as scoring forwards—long as they avoid jumping octaves to deliver some trill and flourish. Mama whites in the audience don't appreciate that kind of standout presumption. Asses squirming the minute any ashy girl starts showing off her pipes.

A little too much GOSPEL influence, Harvey, you know what I'm saying? A few too many amens and hallelujahs filling up this gym.

Mr. Granger just seems relieved he's got a chorus to wave his sad baton at.

Might as well be black as an old white man trying to live on a teacher's salary. Nobody gives a fuck about Mr. Granger. What he thinks, says, eats, drinks, dreams.

Nobody.

The Broomstick pounds over, shakes her head. Not going to fly, whatever his meek suggestion. Overruled. Overpowered. Over and out, man.

Mabel Stallings

Greed and give-me, that's all that Halston bunch knows. Enon coming round with his spittin' image son, pestering me senseless. Hoping, just hoping, I'd keel over in dirt.

Not until I finish teaching Amelia Nell every Halston hook and crook. Not a split second before.

Young'un says she'll be here by noon, then where is she? How long's it take to practice plucking a diploma? Lucian himself said noon and here it is almost three.

"Miz Mabel, how you doing today? You remember my son, Mack, don't you, Miz Mabel?"

Hosing down the zinnias, getting to the peas, was what I was doing and kept doing while keeping a sharp eye on the trespassers.

With Halstons you got to be ever-vigilant. Heat of the day and those buzzards still come circling in a brand new Chevy truck. Tires parked on my grass like Enon already owned what was beneath those rims.

"Mack's part of the business now, Miz Mabel. Loves farming just like his daddy."

"Love money too?"

Heh, heh. Heh, heh.

Fake laughing. False as a fox.

"Nothing wrong with money, Miz Mabel. But you gotta know how to make it. And that tenant farmer of yours, Luther Hodges? He just don't seem to know, now does he?"

"Stupid old cuss."

That got a daddy frown. Next generation don't quite have the hang of Halston smooth.

Yet.

All the while Enon shaking that calculating head of his, like my hedgerows were the saddest sight an eye could behold.

"Ditches, path—none of it cut back since—when? Shame to see 'em looking so ragged. Is that."

Should have turned the hose on them. Run both off with water, if there was water to spare.

"Not enough hedgerows and ditches and field paths of your own, Enon? Got to come round, eyeballing mine?"

Heh heh again. *Heh heh.*

"Got plenty, that's a fact, but I'm a true farmer, Miz Mabel, just like yourself. I see land mistreated, I want to help correct that harm. What I'm proposing would help you too, far as that goes. You and that grandyoung'un you're raising."

After I'm dead and gone and Enon comes after you...

That's when Amelia Nell covers her ears, starts singing nonsense or takes herself elsewhere entirely. Daughters of dead mothers don't warm to dead and dying talk, but I can't give in to squeamishness, not when family property's at stake.

Don't you be getting timid on me, Amelia Nell. I got no use for a timid granddaughter. The management of this farm's gonna fall to you. That's a fact. Like it or don't.

"You think it over, Miz Mabel. We'll talk again."

"Wastin' precious breath, Enon. Yours and mine."

What's he think? Because I got no teeth I got no memory? Last year he laid siege on Luke Jarvis, night and day up at Luke's house, haranguing a man with a wife never cared for farmer tan. Poor Luke didn't stand a chance, battered at from both sides. Soon as he sells to Enon, what happens? Woods fills up with chainsaws, every pine, spruce and beech leveled to stump. And Luke in the worst misery, watching that old growth sink.

Halstons don't believe in windbreaks. Clear-cut every blessed sapling. Cultivate every inch. Not a branch left standing here to Drake's Beach if that family had its way.

I don't ever want a Halston owning what was mine. You understand me, Amelia Nell?

Understood you the first 86 times, Mabel.

Taking me and her heritage no more serious than a chigger bite.

No sir, Enon. I ain't dying yet. Not till that granddaughter of mine learns to love Stallings land much as a Halston loves money.

Calm yourself, Amelia Nell's always saying.

Don't blow a gasket.

Jesus, Mabel, you're, like, PURPLE!

Young'un wants me calm, she'd best get her tail home so I can warn her about the human viper trying to nest in Stallings fields. Get home so her old grandma won't have to stand in a veil of mosquito hawks, sweating up her housedress, straining her neck to see a Ford turn off Bull Run. What's she think? The old got all the time in the world? Time to *waste*?

"Amelia Nell Stallings! Right now, young'un! Get your mess home!"

Clarence

Well now, well now.

Let's stop and be right still a second. Take a moment to reflect.

Cousin Mabel's half blind with mad, Harrison—he sees too much of what's going on around him for a living boy and that ain't something to envy. Certain kinds of knowing don't qualify as gift or blessing, bring misery when they don't bring trouble, and Harrison's in for his share of both. That much I'll tell you flat out. But let's give the mad and the watchful a rest while this hovering spook fills in some facts.

If you ain't figured it out already, I'll say it plain: Harrison Doxey's a good young'un—is and always has been. A little cautious, a little too tied up with what everyone else is doing and feeling, a bit too intent on never stepping in cow pie, but no one who'd run the other way, if a person needed help. That was my impression alive and no cause yet to change that opinion dead.

Been buddies and neighbors since their short pants days, Lucian and Harrison. Made a playground out of our barnyard, the two of them tormenting hens between fighting Indians and dare eating dirt. Loved to shoot down pinecones with Lucian's BB gun, one shot a piece to hit or miss. Jean Doxey wouldn't allow a firearm near her house, but Rosie was a mother thought different. Learned to pick off cottonmouths from the creek bank with a twelve gauge herself, so she saw the sport in shooting, enjoyed it. Boys and guns—that wasn't on my Rosie's fret list. But she'd let loose a yowl every time Lucian ventured close to that Oliver and stretched his big toe to reach the clutch pedal.

Must have been a premonition, the way she distrusted that tractor, suspected it of harm. But since my boy would have slept on that tractor's seat if he could, I figured his pal, given the chance, would feel likewise.

"Climb on up, son. Take yourself a spin."

"No sir," said Harrison, looking every which way but at me. "Un-a. I can't do that."

Mouth saying no, all other parts pleading: *Can I, Mr. Clarence? Can I, no joke?*

By the time he was six, Lucian could out-cuss a sailor. I ain't saying that's good or bad, just saying. Every time as a living man I heard him, Harrison talked clean as a choirboy, polite and proper to a fault, never a foul or filthy word. Even now, rough language don't come natural. He has to think too much, strain in that direction. I ain't saying that's good or bad, just saying.

"Get on up on that tractor seat. Won't hurt a thing."

"My fanny'll hurt plenty when Mama finds out I was driving a white man's machine."

Probably true, but come now: a boy can't run his life doing only what his mama sanctions.

"You think so?"

Joshing, tempting. The devil's got plenty of funning in him, don't you doubt it.

"But she *will*, Mr. Clarence! I know she will."

"Only if she finds out, son."

Harrison looked quick across the field at his own brick house and yard, neat and tidy as a parson's corner.

"I won't tell," Lucian swore, blood-oath solemn. "She won't get it out of me, Harrison."

"That makes two of us can keep a secret. How about yourself? Think you can save your bottom by keeping those lips sealed?"

Big show of teeth was my answer to that, so up he went, Lucian scooting right behind.

Pleased me more than if it'd been my own joy and thrill, watching those two squirts manhandle the steering wheel. Having a good ole time, all three of us, before a porch door slammed mean and here came Rosie, flapping her dishtowel at us.

"Didn't I tell you not to let those boys drive that tractor? Something happens, whose fault will it be?"

"I'm standing right here" was my defense, convinced before events proved otherwise that human had advantage over tractor. "Look at them, Rosie. Ain't hurt or causing it."

Harrison bouncing up and down, trying to body drive that tractor in a barnyard fast as a racecar on a slick track, Lucian sharing his dream.

"Lord a-mercy," Rosie said, appreciating their good time despite herself.

Nothing in that world or this can match my Rosie's lovely grin, eyes bright above it, whole face a dance.

"When those two turn sixteen..."

Didn't finish that thought before I scooped her up for some Carter smooch and nuzzle, Oliver veering toward clothesline pole, Harrison and Lucian and me and Rosie laughing a melody together.

No laughing going on in Cousin Mabel's neck of the woods, seldom is. Grunt and grimace is Cousin Mabel's province—that and sticking like mud to her druthers. Biggest landowner in Mawatuck notwithstanding, Enon and his jug-eared boy should have climbed back into that swanky pickup before they did, passed on strong-arming Cousin Mabel. Cousin Mabel's old but she's still ornery, wild ornery when pressed. If she'd managed to suck a little more air into those overworked lungs, she'd have chased her enemies like a vicious cur down dirt to Bull Run's macadam, jarring awake every swamp critter unwilling to flit about this May day, air heavy as a wool blanket.

Cousin Mabel's hardheaded, you see that. Fierce as a wolverine once she sets her mind on something. Grumping about her granddaughter's stubborn streak like it wasn't her very own pass-along. When what she wants butts cheeks with what is, want comes out ahead. Always has with Cousin Mabel. And what she wants this hour of this day is her granddaughter hearing how Enon Halston presumed himself on

Stallings land a touch before noon, nagging her to rent him what she never will, butcher knife to her throat.

Which her grandyoung'un knows already. Tired of being reminded, what's more. So even if Lucian and Amelia Nell did pull in on schedule, Mabel wouldn't be satisfied. Here's why. Amelia Nell'd take one look at that nose red as Christmas, cheeks puffed out, mouth pinched in, whole package glistening with sweat, and then Amelia Nell'd be the one laying in.

"Way to go, Mabel. Biggest asshole in Mawatuck's whistling cause he got your goat and you're set to explode. "

"Enon Halston didn't get my goat. I got his!"

"Right. I can tell. Remind me to spit and stomp next time I'm celebrating."

Like I said: Mabel Stallings raised and molded. Amelia Nell's been in her grandma's care since before she was teething, so that guardian's influence runs wide as well as deep. Just now the girl's scrappiness mostly shows itself in the vicinity of her trainer, though that won't long stay the case. Cousin Mabel's scrappiness? It ain't all going to fight Enon. That battle takes but a drop of her storehouse, if that. So don't go worrying about Cousin Mabel running out of spunk any time soon. Cousin Mabel's got plenty of spunk to spare, always has.

Harrison

Bored senseless, that's a fact, hot-dull, sleepy-dull, 48 Mawatuck Hornets without the umph to buzz or sting.

The exception being, big no-surprise: Allison Ferrell, prancing round on her spiky heels, making sure people see her prancing, flipping a peroxided curl or two.

The Broomstick knows Allison's tricks. Ought to. After four years.

"Mrs. Bru—uuu—uume! How much LONGER!? It's STIFLING in here."

Well, shit. The Broomstick's more distracted than I thought.

"Just keep your shirt on!" she says.

Just keep your shirt on?

In four years, never has the Broomstick goofed so bad. Boys snapping out of their dozes like switches off a crepe myrtle.

"Naw, naw! Take it off! Take it off!"

Up and scrambling for a better look at the would-be stripper who's just so EMBARRASSED by all the attention, pulling down on her blouse tight enough to show off her nipple knots.

"BACK IN LINE! NOW!"

But Allison's suddenly lost all propulsion, into slink and drag.

"Look at you, drooling. Set to prove what they already believe? Every black man's got to have himself a white bitch?"

"No drool dripping here, Jocelyn. Check again."

Like Jocelyn McPherson will ever believe anything besides what she does, evidence to the contrary or not.

First week of September, '65, first time our blackness, any blackness, rubbed up against Mawatuck High School desks and toilets. Hot then too, but hot with heat that carried the chance of cooling, if you had the patience to wait.

The "first fifteen," our people called us. All of our teachers, the bulk of Central classmates content to stay put, no interest in intermingling, not even slightly inclined to share ball practice and homerooms with the other color. Nobody despised that other color more than Jocelyn McPherson, but whose name appeared first on the transfer sign-up list?

Uh-huh.

Jocelyn's got her version of that first day, I got another. I say all that eyeballing was about scouting the power trail: who led, who followed, both camps. Their side found out soon as Jocelyn stepped off the bus, pushed to the head of our clot and stayed there, nostrils flaring, daring anything white to imply she didn't belong exactly where she stood.

Hoping someone would. Still hoping.

"Hi, Jocelyn," Nell calls over to where Jocelyn presides, too proud to sprawl with the rest of us lowlifes.

"Jocelyn? Hi," Nell calls again, then waves.

Pitiful please-like-me wave.

Doesn't get past Allison.

Un-a.

"Poor Nell. Not even black girls give her the time of day."

"Do you even KNOW how to shut up?"

A question I'd like answered too, but Nell's words sound stringy, wheezy, because this time Allison's meanness hits the mark: Jocelyn can't be bothered by the likes of Nell Stallings, a scrawny, fawning white girl without nerve or gumption to tackle what scares her.

"You're born one or the other. One or the other, Harrison. How long you have to live in this world before you ABSORB that fact?"

Nell's easy to snub, but Jocelyn's been known to make short work of the cocky too. In study hall, Allison and Melinda chattering about class superlatives, "Most Likely to Succeed," "Wittiest," "Most Studious," all those labels invented to fill up a yearbook. Picture of me and Darlene Sawyer inside a hoola hoop for "Most Athletic."

That kind of shit.

But Allison wasn't entirely satisfied with just Melinda's opinion. Decided she wanted Jocelyn's too. Assumed she and Melinda could double-team it out of the black girl.

Cocky.

And dumb.

"Tell us, Jocelyn. Who got YOUR vote for 'Best All Around'?"

Nell and me both eavesdropping. At her leisure, Jocelyn closed her history book, pivoted just a hair to take in Allison, sidekick Melinda not worth addressing. Stared in silence until her questioner started to titter—not because Allison's UNCOMFORTABLE, see, because Allison was convinced the nigger in front of her didn't have sense enough to answer.

I heard Nell take a breath. I probably sucked in some oxygen too, but Jocelyn's face stayed mask. Let Allison's titter wind down. Watched that pale mouth go through its motions.

Should have stayed out of it—Nell. Why didn't she? Half the time she won't defend herself or anybody else, other half she jumps in where she's no use.

"Who cares who anyone voted for?"

"I didn't ask YOU, Nell. I asked JOCELYN."

"But superlatives are a joke! Everybody knows that!"

When Nell shouts, her whole body jerks.

"Allison cares," Jocelyn corrected, calm as a purring cat. "Don't you, Allison?"

Right then, that's the first time Allison might have considered switching tactics.

"Of course I care and so does everybody else."

"Reeeallly?"

That drawn-out word double-dosed in sarcasm.

Second chance for a re-think on Allison's part came, went.

"Do you or don't you intend to say who you voted for?"

"As it happens," Jocelyn said, slow as tweezing splinters, "I voted for one of YOU."

Where's a camera when you need one, man?

If I could have flashed-bulbed Allison's reaction, plastered that gone slack jaw, that *uh-duh-what?* expression, on every bulletin board.... Totally confused, man. Couldn't for the life of her decide if the black girl was telling the truth or putting her on. Nell, shredding her fingernails, just as clueless. And all the while Jocelyn's poker face never changed, not even when she glanced my way.

"Lie or dare?" I asked afterwards, just the two of us, no one else, white or black, listening in.

"Figure it out, Sambo."

Figure it out, Sambo.

Bitch.

Lucian's back again, armpits of his blue shirt three shades darker. Breaks a stick of gum apart and hands half to Nell.

"God almighty, it's hot."

Flapping his shirttail to create a breeze.

"Not THAT hot. What've you been doing? Pushups?"

"Arm wrestling Jimmy Barnard."

"Oh brother."

"Idiot bet me a beer."

"Is this Jimmy Barnard's gum?! !"

"*His* beer. *My* chewing gum. God almighty, girl. Watch where you're spitting."

If I suspected I was chewing gum came out of Jimmy Barnard's pocket, I'd spit too. Jimmy's one of those swamp Crackers who looks like his daddy's also his uncle. Acne craters, chin sharp as a hatchet, eyes so close together there's barely room for nose ridge. Glazed over those eyes, most of the time from weed. Mighty fine weed. Weed Jimmy's happy to sell to any color, long as it's not on credit.

"Rat ugly and stupid as sticks," Jocelyn says of the Jimmy Barnard type. "Got that white skin working for him, though. Better than money in the bank."

But, for instance, take Lucian. White or not, look what he's got to contend with: a crazy daddy set to prove no one's crazier. The Carters living in a house my mama and daddy wouldn't think of calling home. Roof half gone, water pump in the kitchen, not even a spigot. Wood stove for heat, kerosene to see by, outhouse to crap in. Sixty acres of weeds getting weedier, near worthless land even if Clarence did every once in a while use his tractor to cultivate instead of cruise. Lucian's Fairlaine's the most valuable item on that property and without Wayne's junkyard connections Lucian wouldn't have a car at all. Then there's Nell—where's her white picnic? Living in a trailer with a grandmother fierce as Clarence is crazy. Parents dead before she knew them, gurgling their last in Mawatuck Sound.

"OKAY. EVERYBODY. *FINALLY* WE'RE READY."

Good thing too because the Broomstick is looking over the top freaked and frazzled, like if anything else gets between her and wrap-up, she'll pull out a pistol and start firing.

Mr. Granger's perked up, that's a hopeful sign. Mrs. Avery and her clipboard are easing off stage. Potted palms staying put. Even Jocelyn McPherson is joining our snake-line, the Broomstick stationed at its head, hand clamped hard on the senior marshal's arm and counting off.

Every four beats she shoves the next in line out onto plastic that crackles, a stiff-legged parade with the exception of wiggle-ass Allison, giving the boys behind a little show.

"Don't rip the plastic!"

Louder than organ, that Broomstick blast.

Nell wiggles too, wobbly on her semi-high heels.

On cue if not on beat, Mawatuck Rebel/Hornets dividing off, one left, one right, filling up rows of folding chairs.

Then...a gap.

Jocelyn's fencing with the Broomstick, refusing to let those pushy white fingers, teacher-owned or otherwise, dig into her black flesh, direct her entrance. Jimmy Barnard cuts in front of their tussle, jerks his middle finger at the Broomstick's back.

Just us tall boys left, Lucian and me.

"I said PRACTICE for commencement in COMMENCEMENT SHOES!"

"Yes, ma'am. I know you did."

"You are NOT wearing those to graduate."

Pointing at my gold sneakers laced in navy blue—school colors, man!

"Yes ma'am, I am."

Wrench away to kick-strut to my designated seat, the boy rows whistling, clapping.

Even hard-to-please Jocelyn raises a fist in approval, pumping black over blonde.

Clarence

Don't think I take offense at what Harrison says about the ramshackle
Carter farm. Furillo and Jean Doxey wouldn't for a minute consider
calling my house home without some serious upgrades, inside and out,
their own brick ranch built new from the ground up the year before
Harrison came along. Proud as peas over that solid construction and
cultivated yard, every right to be. Not a wayward shrub to be seen, no
blade of grass longer than the next, windowpanes so sparkly bugs go
blind on a regular basis. Hard work keeping a yard and house trimmed
and spotless, and I give Furillo and Jean due credit for the effort. It's just
not the kind of effort I'm familiar with. Carter farmhouse was never
much to brag on, even in Granddaddy's day and it ain't improved. Can't
myself remember when the roof sported more shingles than plywood.
Foundation's always sagged, far as I know. Outhouses, barn, just as
rickety. It's a joking Lord that kept those structures from blowing to
pieces, hurricane after hurricane, but there they stand. He's got some
fun in him, the Lord does, though a lot of his teasing comes with a right
sharp jab.

State of our lodgings, chickens' lodgings, didn't bother me, Rosie
neither. It was Rosie said, our wedding year: "Look at us. So foolish in
love we'd be happy living in a Boy Scout tent." And we would have been
too. The good folks of Mawatuck will tell you I never dropped a bead of
sweat to improve the place or even half tried to keep it up, and I didn't.
Once you watch your own daddy break his back slaving to no good
effect you'd have to be crazier than I pretended to keep at a task so
unrewarding, thirty years on. Every morning, early, Daddy'd step out on
the back porch, pipe clenched between his teeth, studying what
stretched on all sides: dead trees, rotten fences, broken diggers, ribby

cows, wiry fowl. Then he'd set off into the thick of it, do his best to fix what defeated him, day after day after day. Every time he'd get a portion of fence repaired, a cow would walk through a section farther down. Every time he'd get a dead tree branch sawed in pieces, a hard wind would kick up and knock another down. At night, through the floorboards, I'd hear his iron bed frame squeak and squall from tossing and turning, a man hemmed in, nagged at even in dream by all that needed doing, and like the sum of us a man not knowing if he had 40 days or 40 years to set matters straight.

Jean, Furillo, a lot of people in Mawatuck spend time and money caulking chimneys, spraying for termites, greasing combines. That's their privilege, maybe their pleasure. But listen: anybody laboring hard in the here and now, thinking they're booked for eternal rest—facing serious disappointment. Best take a vacation while you still got the breathing body to enjoy it. Because the ever after? It ain't what the preacher promised. The dead can't rest and relax—too much to do, hustling back and forth between the done and about-to-be. Even a lazy crazy fool like Clarence Carter has to keep pace, rush about like those red ants scrambling across Cousin Mabel's toes.

So don't expect to put your feet up, dead.

Ain't gonna happen, friend.

Mabel

Clever skunk.

Enon forcing me to defend Luther Hodges when the man badly needs his draggy ass kicked. Day after day sits perched on that John Deere, engine idling, staring up at puff clouds instead of focused on seed and dirt. Never moves faster than clotted cream. Half that, the minute my back's turned.

Slowpoke or clear-cutter, that's a farmwoman's renting choice in Mawatuck.

I don't glimpse a turquoise fender in the next five minutes, *you're looking at trouble, Missy! Trouble!*

Off lollygagging. Bad as Luther Hodges. Not a thought for her grandma dealing with conniving Halstons on a day too hot for May.

You, yourself, bear the blame, Mabel Stallings, for putting off what shouldn't have been even before Enon started his beg and bow campaign.

Young'un's got to fast catch up now, learn what she ought to know already: farming's serious business, full of surprise and accident, bad years and worse.

"Today young'un! Soon as you get here. Lessons start."

And what hears that sworn oath except a pair of magpies and red ants, swarming these swole ankles?

Stay still too long in Mawatuck, varmints assume you're ripe for the plucking.

Same with a Halston. Very same.

Enon thinks because I'm near dead and my next in line's a young'un, this farm's his for the asking, but that ain't the case. No

Halston plow's gonna slice into Stallings dirt long as this heart slams against bone. Not when it quits slamming, either.

Clarence

If Cousin Mabel would put that fret of hers in motion stead of stomping dust where she stands...

I'm gonna give a little nudge in that direction.

There.

See that?

Head rearing back? Fighting air push?

Alive or dead, no purchase in contradicting Cousin Mabel.

But if she did light out for macadam down her stretch of dirt, not one inch of it bank-owned, pretty soon she'd be inspecting greenbrier and rattanvine, poking at ditch jugging and ditch algae with her walking stick, checking on her hand-lettered NO TRESPASSING signs, fuming less about the girl set to inherit that Stallings territory, free of encumbrance, feeling better whether she intended to or not.

I don't say quit fuming entirely, mind you. That would be closer to miracle than likely. Fussing about her grandyoungun's lollygagging's become second nature to Cousin Mabel. Been complaining about that slowpoke tendency in Amelia Nell since the two of them first traipsed the quarter mile to Bull Run macadam to meet the school bus.

Six-years-young and not a bit school-inclined, Amelia Nell used to try every trick and then some to miss that carriage. Whining, sulking, dragging her feet and book bag and Cousin Mabel not about to let desire become fate.

To understand Cousin Mabel even a little bit, you got to understand the cling and raw between those two, how Cousin Mabel argues with herself about how best to raise a child she never expected to land in her care.

To a morning dozen years back, we're circling now. Amelia Nell scrawny then too, but short scrawny, all elbow and knee, Cousin Mabel's legs not a bit gimpy then, pistons of speed.

First Amelia Nell tries dropping to dirt to retie her shoelaces, already double-knotted back at the trailer by Cousin Mabel who's looking on that unnecessary operation with lips locked, hazel eyes glowering like the god of thunder. Little farther up the road, Amelia Nell's suddenly seized with the need to find the perfect hopscotch piece, gotta have it TODAY, mica or quartz, flat-edged, just so, and that means digging for anything that glints, dirtying up fingernails only lately relieved of yesterday's earth coat. Cousin Mabel's grinding incisors now, giving her jaw a workout while Amelia Nell widens the hunt, scrambling past ditch bank to the mossy edge of swamp, testing out cypress twigs, sycamore balls, pretending there's a chance they'll toss better than rock.

When by hook and crook Cousin Mabel manages to get the girl within sight of Bull Run, Amelia Nell plops her tailbone down for a lunch money recount on the spot.

"Young'un! You're getting yourself filthy as a barn rat!"

"Brood sow you said yesterday."

"And today I'm saying barn rat. Don't be sassing me. Especially with drawers full of grit. Git up before I start yanking."

"But I'm so *winded*!"

Indolence, real or put-on, never has charmed Cousin Mabel.

"Six-year-old giving out before a sixty. Something strange about that state of affairs."

"Think so?" Amelia Nell asks. "How come?"

"Git up now and dust yourself off. We ain't missing the bus to discuss it."

Regardless of those instructions, Cousin Mabel could have boiled a rump roast in the time it took Amelia Nell to rise and pretend-swipe at that grubby bottom.

"Turn around. Let me have a look."

Slower rotation no spinning top ever achieved.

"Uh-huh, well, when other young'uns start pointing and snickering at those black drawers on the playground, I want you to consider what good winded did you."

Amelia Nell gives her grandma the squirrelly eye then, wondering if Cousin Mabel knows something she doesn't, can see the lay of that playground and herself caught somewhere between giant strides and monkey bars, singled out, picked on, that version of events causing Amelia Nell to knock at her behind with a little more spirit because to understand Amelia Nell, you got to understand how a young'un can smart mouth a grandma she's known forever and still shy away from playground spotlight. Six-years-old or eighteen, Amelia Nell keeps to the same strategy. Don't draw attention, avoid undue notice, help people all you can forget you're the daughter of the drowned.

Soon as her grandyoung'un falls into a brood, Cousin Mabel repents. Wishes she hadn't been aggravated to the point of meanness, playing on playground terrors, but it's that very meanness that gets them moving again, gets Amelia Nell to the bus on time, a grandma's duty, whether or not that child cottons to school.

Quarter to three every afternoon, Mabel's again walking that dirt lane to meet that same bus, return loop. About the time it passes Horace and Ophelia Brooks's house, a head pops out a back window. Then a head and shoulders. Then a head, shoulders, flapping arms and ribcage, all belonging to the sprite who'll tear down those bus steps, barrettes lost, sash untied, skin as well as drawers covered with grime.

Day after day bus driver Dwayne says: "Miz Mabel, Amelia Nell's not supposed to be leaning out the window. She knows that."

And day after day Cousin Mabel nods, promises to have a word with the disobedient, won't, because Cousin Mabel believes kin ought to be able to greet kin anyhow they choose, regardless of Dwayne Barco's rules. Comes the afternoon, though, when Dwayne himself is obliged to get off the bus for a set-to with the guardian.

A man-boy weary as a potato sacker, Dwayne is. Even his eyelids look put upon, forced again and again to blink. Nothing wrong with him another job wouldn't cure but the job he's got is driving a wild bunch of brats to school and back nine months of the year, pledged to keep that bunch safe, sound and in one healthy piece.

"Sorry to say, Miz Mabel, Amelia Nell drew blood today."

Eyelids at half-mast.

Cousin Mabel listens, not without sympathy for Dwayne's plight, but, same time, not instantly inclined to take his side.

"Her blood or somebody else's?"

"Else's. Jeremy Smithson to give him a name."

"And how exactly that come about?"

"Bit the boy."

"And why exactly did she do that?" Cousin Mabel quizzes, causing Dwayne to sigh like a man deprived of all aid and comfort.

"I'm the bus driver, Miz Mabel. I'm supposed to be watching the road, not judging fights and how they start."

Amelia Nell, off the bus but not quite so gleeful as usual, sidles close as she dares to that conversation to snoop. No luck. So instead she tries to look as much like a dirt-smeared angel as she possibly can.

Exhaust clouds poot from the exhaust pipe, bus departs, Amelia Nell and Cousin Mabel take off too, Amelia Nell cutting her eyes, checking Cousin Mabel's expression every few steps until finally the suspense proves too much, and she stops short, plants a hand on hipbone.

"You gonna spank me for fighting?"

"You deserve a spanking, Missy?"

"No! But Jeremy Smithson deserved to be bit!"

Since Cousin Mabel stays silent as stars, Amelia Nell tunes up, drips tears.

"He DID, Mabel! I swear he did!"

"Don't recall asking you to swear one way or the other, Missy."

"Okay. But I wish I'd kicked him too."

"Do you now? You intend on saying why?"

Not before she sucks back some of that sniffling. Even then, a fingernail already chewed past tender quick gets gnawed, such actions convincing Cousin Mabel whatever happened on that bus went beyond kid tussling, started with something that might make her want to draw blood herself.

"What? He make fun of you? Your people?"

Maybe the Stallings clan don't count as the richest, and maybe Amelia did make a baby with Harry Dozier, no ring on her finger before or after, but what a Stallings earned he and she earned by dent of skint knuckles, sweat and sacrifice. No shame in that.

Fired up, Cousin Mabel's not as observant as she should be, not as careful either, her grandyoung'un's whole body quivering with distress.

"I can stand here till moonlight. Don't think I can't. Or won't. You'll save us both time and misery answering now what your grandma asked."

"Ma-bel!"

"You heard me, young'un. Start talking."

Mumbles is what she gets. Amelia Nell drawing dirt circles with a scuffed saddle shoe.

"Jeremy was blocking the window."

"I'm listening."

"...And he wouldn't push aside and let me...wave. Like I wanted to."

"Uh-huh."

"Then he leaned out himself."

"Go on."

"And started...saying things."

"Don't make me beg after every sentence, Amelia Nell! Tell what the boy said."

"Don't YOU make ME!"

"You'd rather I pay a visit to Clyde Smithson? Ask HIM what his boy said on the school bus because my grandchild lacks the gumption to say herself?"

An example, if you're looking, of Cousin Mabel shoving too hard and rough, like she does when an obstacle won't give.

"All right! You want to know so bad, I'll tell. He said: "'Look at Nell's mama. She's ugly AND old!'"

Like Wilhelmina Smithson's such a special treat for the eyeballs is the first thought rocketing through Cousin Mabel's noggin. Second is *who's that little pissant calling old?*

"I gave him chance to take it back, Mabel, I did," Amelia Nell starts whimpering. "I even said it twice: 'Take it back, Jeremy!' But when he wouldn't, I bit into him good."

When her grandmamma's scowl veers elsewhere, the confessor takes heart, stretches out a arm and points at what should have been a meaty spot.

"Right here's where I got him."

"Right where? Elbow or farther down?"

"Farther down."

"Hmmp," Cousin Mabel says.

"And, Mabel, listen. You know what else?"

"You got a what else worth repeating?"

"Felt like I hit bone too."

Lickety-split, Cousin Mabel takes off at a trot because she's got a cackle in her throat threatening to ruin all the previous fuss and fume and she can't let her grandyoung'un grow up thinking teeth marks will cure everything that ails. But trotting along, believe you me, Cousin Mabel is pleased as a pig by what she's heard dent of threat.

When a Smithson laid into a Stallings, a Stallings repaid the compliment by laying in right back. And that's exactly what grandma's been preaching every morning, buttering Amelia Nell's breakfast biscuit. *Defend your own.* 'Cause if kin won't stand up for kin, who the hell will?

Harrison

Piling out of that gym like we're being hunted, man: white as well as black.

"What a fucking waste."

"What a fucking DISASTER."

"Lame-o."

"Jesus, I'm starving!"

"Can you believe the sun's still out? Feels like MIDNIGHT."

"Next weekend, all over again, wearing a robe."

"Fuck."

"Can't wait, can you?"

"Fuck."

Melinda, Allison, Jocelyn, Nell, Jimmy and everybody else—united, for once.

"Mabel's going to have a cow. I promised to be back by noon."

Nell whining, Lucian shrugging.

"What're ya gonna do, Amelia Nell? Defy a teacher?"

A little elbow action, my direction. Like it's both of us giving Nell the business.

"Hey, Lucian. Next time invite your old man. We could have used the entertainment."

"Right," Lucian says to that wise guy.

"Right," through a tight little white smile.

Category all their own, man, tight white smiles. Akin to lockjaw. Clamped down, ground down, holding fast.

"Right."

Clarence

A finer woman than my Rosie never there was. To the very last, contrary to public outcry, she held to her opinion, did her damnedest to persuade our boy to share it.

"Your daddy's not seriously touched, Lucian. Crazy's a scheme of Clarence's. A scheme that got away from him, but his scheme nonetheless."

Whether Lucian totally believed his mama—then or now—I can't with certainty say. But the boy invested substantial effort in *trying* to believe his daddy had good sense—which is more than can be said of his grandparents on his mama's side.

If it sounds like I'm badmouthing Lily and Alfred Arnold, holding too tight to a slight, I've got reason. Hard to overlook they never wanted a Carter branch gnarling up their family tree, dead set against a union between Rosie and me, one of them forgetting, the other one resenting, that a daughter in love is first a woman in love.

Back then Rosie and me liked nothing better than taking the bus to Ocean Park for a day in carnie land alongside sailors on Sunday leave. Strolling the boardwalk with our cotton candy swirls, riding rides. Just me and Rosie out of Mawatuck County, beyond invalid Lily's reach.

"Sit, Rosie," I'd say, "and watch your honey pie break this sorry contraption." Then I'd snatch the sledgehammer out of the vendor's hand and slam it hard enough to knock that clang-a-dang bell off its post, shirtsleeves rolled up high so lots of muscle showed.

Ask Rosie and she'll tell it different.

"Yes, Clarence tried to break that bell but he was just as keen on breaking into a sweat that didn't offend."

Repeating that tale to Lucian, she always added on: "Your daddy's peculiar in some ways, but peculiar's not crazy."

At Ocean Park, when a scared stupid rider got caught at the top of the ferris wheel, howling and begging for operator mercy, we'd join the gawkers eyeing that spectacle. Then we'd mosey over to the Twister, where the howling never stopped, each car spinning two directions at once, grown men green with fear. After that, at least once a trip, we'd pay a visit to the Fun House where I'd have to haggle for a ticket. "These tiny boats won't support a substantial gentlemen like yourself," the concessionaire would warble, and I'd have to use my heft to bargain, leaning in close, crowding the little man. Rosie did her part in persuading too. "Are you DENYING us a ride, sir? I wouldn't think that would be good for business. Especially since we've got all day to walk around, sharing our disappointment."

Sly one, ain't she?

Couldn't sit on the same seat as Rosie, ticket or no ticket, the two of us just wouldn't fit, so she'd settle in front and lean against my knees. Boat prow would bump open the swinging doors and slosh us into a darkness wet and humming, walls dripping on either side, whole route smelling like a flooded cave. At each turn a yellow light popped on to show a ghost or goblin such as the living imagine, moldy puppets that shouted "boo." Near the skeleton's corner was where I first reached inside Rosie's nylon blouse to stroke a nipple that rose to greet me and, the Lord be praised, didn't get that exploring hand slapped away. But just to make sure I hadn't misjudged her pleasure, confused it with mine, back in the boardwalk's light I checked every inch of that gorgeous face. Not a frown or hint of one brewing could I see, which shook loose a giggle in me that didn't quit till Rosie hushed it with a kiss.

After the pier lights winked on, last ride of the day, we'd amble over to the roller coaster. Wobbly as a homemade fence, those wooden cross-struts, but we took our chances along with the rest of the drunk and sober for the thrill of dip and dive. Much as I liked the look of Rose

Arnold head to toe, green eyes and rump of plenty, I had to make sure I wasn't wooing a nervous, skittish woman. Had to prove to myself and maybe her too that those fine features came with a core tougher than her sickly mama's, no sense in it for either of us if not. Carters, by blood or marriage, are a grin and grit variety. Start out that way, or adapt.

"Not scared are you, Rosie?" I one Sunday shouted against manufactured wind.

Fingers wrapped tight around the metal bar that penned us, knuckles white as bed sheets, my Rosie replied just as loud: "Scared of a rinky-dink RIDE? Not this girl."

Ah Rosie. Don't I miss the flesh of that woman, the bound and determined loyalty that lovely flesh padded. Lily and Alfred Arnold might have objected to their only child marrying a slaphappy Carter, throwing herself away on a man with the ambition of a flea, but once Rosie made up her mind it was made up. She meant to call me husband.

I see her now, climbing those carpeted stairs, carrying her mama's supper tray, a spray of violets beside the ham and beets Lily won't so much as sample. Lily propped on crocheted pillowcases, reigning supreme from her sickbed, Rosie entering that chamber of mama's wants and wishes with some wants and wishes of her own.

Balances that tray on the bedside table, tucks in a corner of her mama's blanket before declaring: "I'm marrying Clarence, Mama."

"Do it, and break my heart, Rosalee."

A girl grows up with such a mama as Lily presiding, she learns some maneuvers of her own.

"Your heart's already broke, Mama. That's what you said. The first time I left the house with Clarence."

"There's broken that heals and broken that stays broken," Lily says and starts coughing feeble, hoping to cough up a speck of blood, trying every trick to make her usually obedient daughter stay that way. And maybe Mama Lily would have gotten her way again if me and Rosie hadn't already found ourselves a private spot in the mulch of Gull's

Landing, become acquainted inside out. A mama's needs won't ace a woman's, no matter how dutiful the child.

Alfred, he's waiting his turn downstairs in the parlor, sitting straight in a hardback chair, a man denied comfort so long he scarcely remembers what he's missing. Bald as the moon, spectacles sitting crooked on his nose, Alfred's long been trying to prevent upset and upheaval in his household on doctor's orders, but this bright noon he's trying for reasons closer to his heart.

"That farm Clarence inherited won't bring in more than four thousand on a good year, Rose. Less, I'm afraid, on average."

I don't blame Alfred for laying out what his daughter could expect, money-wise, twining fates with me. That's part of a daddy's job come wedding time.

But now that I can go back and join them in that room, I see the 4000 figure distresses my Rosie more than she's willing to admit to daddy or herself.

"We'll rent other land. Make up the shortfall."

"Renting takes money too, Rose. People don't lend out land for free."

"Then we'll find another way."

Flying hot, sharper with her daddy than she means to be because his is the second objection she's heard, two too many.

Alfred falls silent, bald head slumping.

I pay too much attention to head hair, Rosie says. Stuck on the subject. But the day that tractor flipped on me, my thatch was still thick as crabgrass. Vanity bragging maybe, but true.

Second date I said, straight out: "No need to worry about this head ever going bald. I come from a long line of bushy-headed Carters."

"Been living with bald all my life. What makes you think I care about lost hair?"

"Because you been living with bald all your life."

When a laugh sneaks up on Rosie, her whole face shows the surprise, temples, chin, gums. And she was tickled with my head hair, I can tell you that. A woman who'd just as soon stroke a pate as yank curls is a woman cool to other things about a man in his prime, I guarantee.

"I love Clarence and I'm going to marry him—whatever you and Mama have to say about it."

"The carpentry business can't support two families just now. I wish it could, but it can't."

Not with a stack of medical bills the likes of Lily's to pay. A wagon train of doctors in and out of that house every week and none of those visits cheap.

"Much as I'd like to, I can't offer Clarence a job. I just don't have the money to hire a helper."

Hardly through with that sentence before my bride-to-be flares up again.

"Clarence and I don't need charity, Daddy. Yours or anybody else's."

Says it because she believes it. Believes young and healthy and in love is enough, more than enough, to solve, conquer, beat back any problem that comes knocking. Wouldn't trust anyone, related or strange, warning her right then blunt as beans: *Darling child, it's the problem you're fixing to marry. It's the problem you'll be cuddling with in that marriage bed.*

Never one for bluntness, Alfred accepts with grace what can't or won't be changed. Kisses his daughter's cheek, tries to look less pained than he feels.

"You're my daughter, Rose. Helping you and your husband when I can won't be charity."

Said it before, say it now I got no quarrel with Alfred. He had my Rosie's best interests at heart, delivered harsh truth gentle, and when she ignored his counsel never once threw it in her face that she'd been cautioned. Came to visit us regular, treated me courteous, slipped Rosie spending money when he thought I wasn't looking, careful not to offend, overstep. A father-in-law welcome in my house, first to last.

Mama-in-law Lily was another matter. Search low or high, you won't find many Lily defenders in Mawatuck. Thinks no one's fancy enough in the county for her to call equal or friend and Mawatuck repays the snub in full, no fan of the invalid's. The woman wants to put on airs, so be it. That's her business. But expecting the rest of us to bow and scrape to the queen? That's pushing it.

Once and only once did she rouse herself from her crocheted pillowcases to make the trip up Carter lane. Rosie's the one answered the door to that vision in mourning black, pale cheeks powdered paler.

Came to verify, she announced, if the "vicious" rumors could possibly be true: her only daughter living without benefit of running water.

"Oh our water runs, Miss Lily, you pump long and hard enough."

Didn't provoke a grin, that correction. Didn't expect it would.

"*Never* did I think I'd live to see this day."

Probably not, since she'd been on her last legs, at death's door, signing the roll called up yonder, for a dozen years at least.

"Look at this face, Mama. Does this look like the face of a suffering woman?"

And what could a professional sufferer like Lily Arnold reply, staring at bright-eyed, pink-cheeked evidence to the contrary, her daughter looking in every pore like what she was: a bride well and soundly loved?

"But you're living like...like..."

"Poor white trash? Is that what upsets you, Mama? Afraid people are calling your daughter poor white trash?"

Lighting kerosene lamps, hiking out to a privy, feeding wood to a potbellied stove. We did all that and didn't fuss about it. Why'd we need electricity and indoor plumbing? We had something better: each other's love and company night and day. Got along fine, better than fine, Rosie and me and once Lucian was born, Rosie and me and the child we made. And that getting along fine would have continued if the government hadn't sent a posse to collect its cut of the piddling profit sixty acres brought in.

Rosie hanging clothes in the side yard, Lucian and Harrison playing nearby. Me at the kitchen sink, taking care to wash every part of myself twice because a big man needs a lot of cleaning, summertime, especially.

While he was still peeing in his diapers, Lucian's mama set him straight on that score too: "Your daddy's a big man, but he's a clean man."

And I was, stripping down twice a day to lather up.

But the sink window faces field and Jean and Furillo's house, not Carter lane.

From this angle and distance, I feel right sorry for that bathing fella, don't you? Humming a tune, blind and dumb to the nuisance and mischief circling round his weeping willow, about to ease to a full stop next to a bashed can of kerosene. Once upon a time he'd led a simple, peaceful life. Good one, too.

Mabel

Wash what hair's left to this head on Sundays, whatever the Edna Dowdys have to say about it. My Lord's the same as Edna's and he's got nothing against his creatures getting clean when they can fit in getting clean.

Why not cut off 10 inches and save yourself some trouble?

Thin and straggly mess—but mine. To keep.

Your old grandma ran from everything that caused her trouble, she'd have herself a bunch of nothing. A bunch of NOTHING, Amelia Nell!

Instead of fighting through bumblebees to save pepper plants from beetle teeth, I'd be spread on a church pew like Edna, thinking I'd finished my day's work.

Gardens are the Lord's house too, full of obligation. Beans to string, tomatoes to fertilize, beets to weed, raccoons to trap. And right next to garden, yard grass to mow, leaves to rake, bushels of pinecones to gather. None of it fond of neglect. Was the time jays and starlings lent assistance, hungry for beetle fat. But why hunt dinner when it's been laid out by Edna and her set? Cracked corn and fancier grain. Overly fond of air fowl, Mawatuck women, treating those fly-ins to birdfeeders, birdbaths, birdhouses on a pole. Never seen a flock of birds didn't herald something bad: bad news, bad weather, bad times. Half hour before the twister tore through Sutter Davis's barn, two by fours smashed like kindling, army of blue-black grackles strutted across my grass, gleaming like they'd been oiled by the devil himself. Omen, if I'd known how to read it. Mawatuck farmers used to worry about hurricanes, northeasters, ice storms and droughts. Now we've got another dread to add to the list, courtesy of Halston clear-cuts: black wind funnels, blowing in, hitting down, destroying what it took a lifetime to build.

Dozen grackle armies wouldn't do justice to the warning Enon's on his way. Him and his sick-making yes and no ma'aming.

What's the big deal? The man can want to rent the farm, but he can't DO it, unless you let him.

More proof Amelia Nell needs schooling on Halston conniving.

When finally she drags herself home yesterday, is she concerned about that trespasser and his schemes?

Won't talk a thing but sunhats.

A million degrees, two sunhats right next to the door, but Mabel Stallings decides to stand bareheaded, glaring down a dirt road. Don't you wish you had a grandma this stubborn, Lucian?

Like Lily Arnold would recognize sun if a fiery ball of it rolled into her shuttered room.

I see Cousin Mabel's out here bareheaded. I see that.

Grinning too much like his daddy to suit my taste, but you can't hold grinning against a boy. He looks after his mama. Crazy daddy too.

Two sunhats on hooks, another five stashed under the bed, but will she take the time to slap one on her head?

I wouldn't be bringing slap into this, I was you.

Though I never raised a hand to the young'un. Pinched her when she needed it, but in eighteen years she's not been slapped by me or anybody else.

Humor the girl, Cousin Mabel. We've lived a day of torment.

And what have I lived, waiting on two young'uns claimed they'd be here by noon?

Sleeping now. Snoozing away the finest part of morning, one heel shot out from the covers, hair like current-caught seaweed in a built-in trailer bed.

Thirty-year cover of ivy and jasmine, wisteria, honeysuckle and every other creeper known to God, and still this tin box glints and steams, blighting the eye and the land it sits on.

How come we live in a trailer, Mabel?

No older than five first time she asked.

How come we don't live in a house?

Your people didn't roll in off a highway, Missy. We had a farmhouse. Built by your great-granddaddy Caleb with Stallings timber.

A house like Lucian's?

Couldn't countenance that comparison even for the sake of kin. Rose Arnold Carter, delirious with love, might see paradise with a privy, but the rest of us see squalor and nothing but.

I said a farmhouse built solid. Painted too.

Solid but no match for a grease fire that jumped frying pan to curtains, racing up the wall and through the ceiling. Autumn wind took it house roof to hay loft, down the orchard path, crabapple, peach, pear and fig trees, entire scuppernong arbor, scorched and singed. Dawn showed rafter cinders, tree roots smoking, two stark chimneys, dish shards, one half-melted hairbrush to break the heart all over again. Amelia and me standing in ash, sniffing it, reminded by that ruin how quick what we called ours could get snatched away. That first lesson by fire, water lesson coming.

Mabel, Mabel? Could our trailer BURN?

If it did, I'd probably dance a jig. But me laughing at the prospect was a mistake, knew that soon as the young'un let loose a jackdaw screech and grabbed at wall paneling like it was a piece of the Lord's ark.

Another lesson. Mock what a child attaches to young and risk that child losing the inclination to attach altogether. Amelia Nell needs to love a trailer on the way to loving the ground it sits on, so be it.

Land, Amelia Nell. Protect it. Cherish it. Treat it like it's your bread and water. 'Cause in Mawatuck County, that's what it is.

Even when field rows look sorry as this. Corn crop pitiful, soybeans worse, leaves pale, stalks runty, plants struggling to live in dirt drier than stripped bark. Not a yard hose big or long enough anywhere to bring relief to these acres. The Lord's got to do it or no one.

"Mabel Stallings! You in a feud with sunhats?"

Hear her before I see her, sprawled on the steps in her nightgown, twirling a sunhat in rebuke, those scabby, mosquito-bit legs about half the size they ought to be.

Wouldn't you think Mabel Stallings would feed her own grandyoung'un?

Edna Dowdy, plenty others, probably been sniping that nonsense behind my back for years now 'cause the young'un does have the look of a starving cat, despite being fed biscuits with pork gravy, peas swimming in butter and ham grease. Those Dozier-side arms and legs of hers get plenty of nourishment, they just refuse to show it. Shaped nothing like her mama, nothing like a Stallings. Stallings women come all-over plump: arms, bosoms, calves. Take away a certain lip pout and eye crinkle and Amelia Nell bears no resemblance to the woman who bore her, looks or attitude. My daughter couldn't get enough of the mirror, granddaughter won't touch a comb unless it's shoved in her hand. Brown as creek water and limp as cooked noodles, Amelia Nell's hair, wet or dry. Gap between her front teeth big enough to stuff a toothpick through. You think the young'un cares? Not a bit. Up till high school wore whatever I laid out for her to wear, now lives in dungarees. And that time I gave her money to buy something that didn't look, smell or hang like denim, something new, what did she wail?

NEW? Nobody buys new anymore!

Make a trade then. I've seen all of that outfit I want to see.

A dress, Mabel? A DRESS?

Like I'd suggested a ball and chains.

Graduation rule or there wouldn't right now be a white dress hanging in the closet in need of hemming. Opposite of her mama that way too. Amelia Nell will still buckle to a rule.

If this is about sex, don't bother.

Well aren't you the wonder? No need for Grandma to share the details then.

Didn't say EVERYTHING. Just enough.

And what's enough, Missy?

Enough to avoid babies.

More than her mama knew, twelve and older. But if I'd run Amelia through a similar quiz, if Amelia'd been more cautious, cared more what people had to say, if she'd put off bedding Harry Dozier, my grandyoung'un would have drowned in Mawatuck Sound along with them, half-formed in her mama's belly or not even spawned, and then where would I be? No blood kin left to will this farm to, no Stallings to keep it Stallings.

"Mumbling to yourself, I hear you. See what happens when you won't wear a sunhat two days in a row?"

"I'm drying my hair, young'un. Won't dry through straw."

"Uh-huh. Except it's bone dry."

"Shush."

"And probably has been for hours."

"Quit your mouthin' and shove over on that step. Give this tired old woman room to sit."

"Start working before dawn, worn out by noon."

"Better worn out than snoozing."

"News flash, Mabel. It's no sin to sleep. Some people actually enjoy it."

Not if they dream water. See your only child in it, trapped and sinking. Off that night to The Lido, leaving me their infant to feed and diaper. "Go to bed when you want, Mama," Amelia called from the Chrysler she'd die in. "I'll check on the baby when I come home." Good time, my Amelia was after, her and Harry too, their daughter sound asleep before they'd turned out of the driveway, but awake I stayed, full of piss and vinegar, rehearsing a speech on obligation I never got to give the party girl. Her and Harry, sideswiped on Mawatuck Bridge, sailing with that Chrysler through splintered railings, sailing, then sinking. Tablecloths, scatter rugs, bud vases, anything the color of Mawatuck Sound or close to, I threw on the trash pile, couldn't stand to have that shade of drowning blue nearby. But nothing I did or could do would resurrect my young'un—for me or Amelia Nell. What the highway patrolman told me, standing on my steps in morning fog, I repeated to Amelia Nell soon as she was old enough to understand.

Mabel, if that woman, you know, my mama, wasn't really dead, just maybe off somewhere visiting and decided to come back? To get me? You know what I'd tell her, Mabel?

You finished with that chicken leg? Don't look half-eaten, backside.

I'd say: Un-a, Mama. You go on back where you came from. I'm staying right here. With Mabel.

How's a grandma supposed to chide that?

"You plan on sleeping twenty-four hours a day once that diploma's curled in your hand?"

"I smell a trick question."

"No trick. But I'm tired of waiting for news without prompting."

"Are we talking jobs or what?"

"A job's a start."

Shrugs, like: *What's it matter?* "I was thinking I might try The Croatan."

"Come again."

"The Croatan. Down at the beach. I hear they're short on waitresses."

"I'm talking more than summer employment, Missy."

"So am I. The Croatan stays open year-round now. Plenty of hungry tourists these days, winter and summer."

"Hustling tables at fifty. That's a fine prospect."

"Fifty? Jesus! Who said anything about fifty? That's FOREVER from now."

Not a clue fifty'll be upon her, seventy too, before she can wipe her nose twice. Stiff joints and heartburn, memory like a sieve. Teenagers think they've got all the time in the world to pick and choose, try out the lot before jumping in.

"We ain't done with this discussion, Missy."

"Yeah, yeah. Sit here and stew while I finish watering."

"In your gown tail?"

"You think the hose cares?"

Right then, a rumble, coming from Bull Run direction. Amelia Nell hears it, same as me. Twists around for a better listen, same as me.

Not the hit and miss of Luther's worn-out pickup, wind-out too smooth for a claptrap truck, smooth as an engine still on warranty.

Coming from the south, closing in.

Twice in two days.

Record, even for Enon.

"Fucking hell."

Enon Halston on the way I don't have time to correct language filth.

"Mabel, Mabel, listen to me. *Listen to me.* That asshole is NOT going to rile you again today. Okay, Mabel? Okay? *Promise me.*"

"Good Sunday morning, Miz Mabel, Amelia Nell."

"Was."

Glaring never sent a Halston scurrying, but this one's glared at, regardless.

"About to have yourself a graduation, aren't you, girl?"

"That's what they tell me."

"Glad to be through with those books for a while, I reckon."

Answer a Halston or not, he'll keep yakking.

"I apologize for stopping by so early. Amelia Nell still in her nightclothes and ya'll fixing to have breakfast, I imagine. But I wanted to make sure Amelia Nell heard my offer to clean up those hedgerows and clear out those ditches. At a price Luther'll never pay for the privilege."

Not everything's about money, Enon. Didn't your mama teach you nothing?

Here's the thing, Enon. It just don't suit my fancy to have every field in Mawatuck tilled by the same man, whatever his name.

You listening with both ears and a gut, Enon? Before I'd rent to a Halston, I'd sooner sell to a developer. And before I'd sink that low, I'd swallow arsenic.

Get off my property, Enon. Get the hell off now!

Can't get it out, none of it, not a word. Tongue thick as sausage, ears roaring.

"Mabel's farm, Mabel's decision. And Mabel says no."

"Uh-huh, but here's the thing, Amelia Nell, you got a stake in this deal too."

Deal.

Calling my land a *deal* to my face.

"Me, I hope and pray Miz Mabel outlives us both, but that's not likely to happen, is it? Us speaking truthful?"

"Nobody's dying, Enon. So why don't you take your mouth and your new shiny truck elsewhere."

"Like I said, Amelia Nell, Miz Mabel, I hope she's blessed to live to a hundred and five, but..."

"Nobody's dying! *NOBODY!* Got that?"

Except something less than life is pressing hard and rough of a sudden, pushing this old woman toward dirt and dandelion, running Mabel Stallings faster to ground than a thieving Halston.

Clarence

Since Enon'll never get one inch of slack from a Stallings, even after saving Mabel a head wallop, in all fairness I have to take up for the man a speck, speak a little in his sorry defense. Worst son of a bitch ever showed his scales, Mawatuck Enemy #1, according to Cousin Mabel, and Enon not putting the effort he should in countering that reputation with her or the rest of the county.

Cash in the bank, land in your name—neither one necessarily makes for a happy man. Enon can't venture out without resentment steaming up, all sides. And he feels it, sure he does, burns him too, because he thinks by consolidating the little, low-yield farms, shaping up fields with high-grade fertilizer and hybrid seed, he's single-handedly keeping Mawatuck in the farming business, protecting it from the very developers Mabel claims she'd call in right after dipping into arsenic. In his own head, see, Enon's just as eager as Cousin Mabel to keep Mawatuck free of Virginia sprawl, six houses to the acre, each one the very same down to where the toilet piddles.

But public ignorance of his good motives ain't what's giving the man ulcers. That honor belongs to son Mack. Besides being nothing pretty to behold, the boy's dumb as a brick and not likely to turn smarter, twenty-five years old, content to ride shotgun in Enon's pickup ten hours a day and never once ask a question about the fields he's riding through. Not a smidgen of interest in his daddy's work, despite Enon's desperate brag. Yep. Mack's the worm eating at Enon's peace of mind because Enon's not the idiot his offspring is. Enon knows he's clothing and feeding and sheltering the very ne'er-do-well who'll squander what it took several generations of Halstons to hoard, squander the whole of it and be surprised by the ruin. That's what Enon lives knowing, day in, day out.

Fathers and sons, grandmas and granddaughters, constant pull and tug.

Not so peaceful around my house Sunday either. While Cousin Mabel's going lightheaded and Amelia Nell's springing at Enon like a cheetah, I'm on my Oliver, puttering toward a spot of quiet and birdsong, pondering ways to bamboozle my aggravating government. More work than it might seem, keeping up the front of harmless crazy. Can't all at once convince people you're a nutcase, because once it's established fact, who's going to notice? See what I'm getting at? You gotta build and stagger revelations to keep folks interested.

So I grabbed an anvil out of Morris Denton's truck bed at the feed store and swung it round a bit. Showed my meat and potatoes to Miz Rainey. Chatted regular with my invisible pal, called by name of Amos. Told Independence Day fortunes from a card table alongside the beach road so superstitious Virginians headed for sand and scorch could take advantage of my forecasting same as Mawatuck folks. Exception of the anvil swinging, I steered clear of serious violence for good cause. Mawatuck's got a long, honorable tradition of pitying and praying over harmless crazies. Never sent anyone less than dangerous to themselves or others off to a padded lockup. Long as I caused federal headaches without terrifying locals, I had leeway in playing peculiar. But I still had to narrow down the possibilities, fix on one and figure out how to get it done, and that required planning. That's the reason I'm out in the fields, morning of Sis's visit. Didn't set out to avoid my kin but ain't a bit sorry I did. Irene's blood but, Lord help her and me, she's someone never knows when to leave or shut her mouth. Oblivious to people in a strain. Won't take a hint or flat-out order to be gone. People tolerant of the lone and lonely might show Sis a quarter hour's sympathy. Then it all comes down to stamina. Hers and yours.

My Rosie pretends to listen to her sister-in-law, contradicts less than she might. Lucian's less accommodating.

"And where's that brother of mine? Man needs to eat as much as Clarence, I'd think he'd be at this table, napkin tucked, making short work of these eggs and bacon strips."

Since Rosie can fry eggs blindfolded, one arm in a sling, been making breakfast since she was knee high for that taskmaster mama of hers, egg whites cooked just so, bacon crisp not burnt, that full-on attention she's giving the frying pan—not strictly required.

"I'm not sure where Clarence took himself off to this morning, Irene. But if you stand on the back porch and holler, he'll probably hear you."

Probably would have, which is far from saying I'd have answered.

"Stand on a porch, bellowing like a washerwoman for my own *brother*!?! What's got in to you, Rose, suggesting such a thing?"

Still playing at dainty, but the scent of sunny-side-ups sliding around in bacon grease is getting harder to resist. Sis *thinks* she just snuck a nibble of bacon, but she was seen by more than a hovering spook.

"Have some breakfast, Irene."

"No, shug, no. I'm still full as a tick from supper last night. Plus this dress shows every little spill and I aim to keep it good for Sundays."

Last night's supper was a can of tomato soup, but never mind. Girl got a brother big as me, she's wary of bread and pork overload. That polka-dotted wonder she claims to be protecting? Bright blue balls bouncing across her shoulder blades, down her ribcage? Not entirely becoming.

"It's a lovely dress," my Rosie compliments.

Reflex talking.

Eyebrows far north, Lucian glances at his mama.

"Master Lucian, you're mighty quiet this morning."

"Air space all filled up."

"Loo-shun."

"Lucian, what? And what are you talking about air space for, nephew?"

What are you talking about anything for? Lucian's thinking, watching Sis snatch another strip of bacon, fear of fat and polka-dot smudge notwithstanding.

"Let me fix you a proper plate, Irene. You want some toast too?"

"And be late for Sunday School?"

"Better get on the road, auntie. Wouldn't want to miss that blessed are the meek Bible lesson."

"I got time yet."

"You like that new preacher, then?"

Rosie again, making idle conversation.

"The Lord wants me in church, so I go, but if it was up to me, I'd never darken the doors again. Everybody whispering about Clarence, speculating what he'll pull next. Clucking, saying: *'Innit a shame, Irene? Innit turrible?'*"

"What's *turrible* is you listening to that crap."

"That's your solution, nephew? Turn a deaf ear? Think that'll help, do you?"

"No help needed."

"For mercy sake, Rose, correct the boy!"

"Nothing to correct. Daddy's fine."

"*Fine?*"

No such thing as shrieking dainty. Even if Sis had a coach.

"And when did that daddy of yours turn the corner and brush up against fine? Because the Clarence I know hasn't ventured near that quarter in quite a spell. *Quite a spell.*"

As much as he's itching to scoop up that piece of birdy kin and Buick stuff her, Lucian looks first to his mama, Rosie steady gazing past both squabblers out the kitchen window toward the back porch.

"No reason to hide the truth from *me*. Clarence's only sister. His full blood kin."

"How many ways do I have to say it? Nothing to hide. Everything's peachy keen."

"*Family*, nephew! With rights on my side and obligation on yours to tell me exactly when and where you last laid eyes on your roaming daddy."

"Climbing out of bed. Lacing up brogans."

Ain't so. Thick in dream, Lucian was, when I left the house.

"So you're prepared to swear he's not this minute running naked through Mawatuck?"

"Repeating himself? You know Daddy's partial to variety."

"What I *know,* Lucian Leviticus, and *you* know and Rose here knows better than the both of us, is your daddy's lately partial to doing the Carter name damage."

"What? No tears to go with that? Usually at flood stage by now."

"If I had any tears left, nephew, they'd be pouring down these careworn cheeks. But your Aunt Irene's all cried out."

"Uh-huh."

"It happens."

"Uh-huh. But will it last?"

Lock that pair in a room and they'd bicker the livelong day. Fresh-mouthed, touchy, can't get along. Never could. Even as a baby, Lucian squalled at the sight of his Aunt Irene, clothespinned his nose when she brought her cloud of Evening in Paris near. On Sis's side, she's been having to crane her neck to chat with Lucian since he was nine. Looking up to a *young'un.*

"This very morning I plan to ask the preacher for counsel, confess how Clarence's gotten worse..."

"He's not WORSE!"

"He stripped *naked* in front of Miss Rainey! Mawatuck's talked of nothing since."

"Let them talk. He didn't hurt the old bat."

"Didn't hurt her!? Nearly scared that poor widow to death. She's 86 years old."

"But lived to tell the tale a million times."

Bullying Lucian's getting her nowhere, so Sis zeroes in on Rosie.

"Rose, listen to me. We were lucky this time, us Carters. Miss
Rainey pressed no charges. Called Donnie Anderson every night for a
week to complain, but pressed no charges. Next widow Clarence strips
in front of might not be so obliging. Meanwhile, look at the bunch of
us. Worried sick over what he might do next. I myself haven't had a
solid night's sleep since February. Bags under my eyes, bowels in an
uproar."

Since Rosie's still looking out the window, giving no sign of hearing
or answering, Sis pulls out all the stops, Sunday dress be damned. Off
that chair, on her knees, freckled arms wrapped tight around Rosie's
shins, burping up one of those sobs Lucian's long expected to hear.

Missed her calling, Sis did. If she'd taken that act to a tent in a
sinner's cornfield, she'd be a certified revival star.

Works, though. No way for Rosie to ignore that clutch.

"Irene, get up now. Come on, hon, get up. You'll mess up your
dress."

"I'm sorry to add to your burdens, Rose, just as sorry as I can be, but
we've got to think. We've got to plan. Things can't go on like this.
Something's got to be done."

Much as I'd like to blame Sis, she's not the only one bothering
Rosie. Those tiny lines cross-etching my darling's face? My doing, I
realize now. And don't it hurt my selfish soul to see that suffering.

"You hear what I'm saying, Rose? Somebody's got to take charge."

That's the last line she mews out before Lucian yanks her up and off
his mama.

"Not *you,* Irene. Got that? Not YOU."

"Put Irene down," Rosie says the way she'd order a dog with a hen's
neck in its mouth.

"Inside that Buick's where I'll put her down."

"Lucian. Mind me."

And he does, he does. Doesn't like minding his mama this moment
but does.

"Irene, hon, I remember now. Clarence went to check on those back ditches for trapping."

Wife and son both reduced to lying on my account, Carter ditches long since trapped out.

"You go on to church. I'll tell Clarence you stopped by. He'll probably come visit this afternoon. Would that suit? This afternoon?"

"I'm not leaving this house—and keep your hands clear of me, Lucian Leviticus!—till I personally speak to Clarence."

Polka-dots in a ruffle, freckles flaming, Sis ain't budging. Lucian tries another hoist, she'll use elbows, teeth if she has to, to fend him off.

"When my only brother needs aid and assistance, the Lord understands a church skip."

"Jesus fucking Christ! Do the Lord and the rest of us a fucking favor, Irene. Get a fucking life!"

Hold it.

We've got to break away for a minute or three.

Cousin Mabel's coming to.

Clarence

"She'll be all right now. The heat's to blame, I suspect," Enon says, slump-shoulder because he can't stand upright in Cousin Mabel's trailer without knocking into a hanging houseplant.

He and Amelia Nell together lugged Cousin Mabel up the steps and stretched her out on that built-in dwarf's couch. Stripped off her old woman shoes, slapped a wet washcloth to her crown.

"Just the heat," Enon repeats, hoping Amelia Nell will agree, ease him of some guilt, but every particle of that young'un is dedicated to bringing Cousin Mabel out of her swoon, fanning her grandma's face double-time with a *National Geographic*, Enon Halston, his guilt, no significance whatsoever in this moment of Amelia Nell time, her every fear of lost and gone magnified a hundred fold.

Eyes open, Mabel can't immediately steady the focus, ceiling moving like a wave above her. Last thing she remembers, she stood nose to armpit with her enemy, pine trees and mimosa for a backdrop.

"Don't crowd her!" Amelia Nell snipes.

Too late.

Mabel sees him for sure now. Who he is. Who's cozied up inside her very home. Knocks aside that *National Geographic*, fighting to stand.

"There you go," Enon says. "She's herself now."

"What the hell you in my trailer for?"

"I'll explain later, Mabel. Lay back down."

"I ain't laying down with a Halston circling."

"Will you *please* just go *AWAY*?"

"What are you saying 'please' to a Halston for?"

"Mabel, relax."

"Relax, nothing. There's a Halston in my house."

"Yep, she's all right now. Just got a little overheated. No surprise about that, May this hot."

Clarence

Sis Irene, she ain't quite exited either. But some of those spraying tears are genuine now.

Tired, tired. Even my Rosie's voice.

"Apologize to Irene. Lucian, you heard me. Apologize to your aunt."

"No need, Rose," Irene says, tapping at heart-level polka-dots. "I'm just going to pretend such words never left my nephew's mouth. People can be hurtful in their worry. If the Lord forgives, so can I."

Lucian's out to protect his mama, but he's going about it the wrong way with Irene. You gotta bob and weave with Sis, temper won't scare her off.

Rosie can usually handle Irene and every other pure and mixed-breed Carter, but on occasion Carters simply aren't susceptible to persuasion. When she takes hold of Irene's freckly wrist, murmuring about improvement, how much calmer and more contented I've come to be, Sis reclaims those freckles, gravely, gravely insulted.

"Maybe I'm not a wife and mother like you, Rose, but I'm not ignorant. And I resent to the core you talking to me like I was. I grew up with Clarence, spent as many years beside him as you have, and when he gets a thing on his mind, it stays put till he's finished with it. So don't try telling me he's through battling the government. Don't. If he's not this very second out there doing mischief, he's scheming it. Bank on it."

So Sis is not without her insights. We're kin and we're alike. Awful alike in some ways.

"So I say again: the three of us have got to put our heads together, figure out a way to put something, keep something, between Clarence and mischief."

"Like what? Tie Daddy up in the barn? Strap him down on a daybed in the attic? Have Mama at his side twenty-four hours a day just so you won't see his ass in the wind? Just so YOU won't be embarrassed?"

"What about your mama? What about *you*? Your own daddy playing slow in public, inviting people to call him crazy and worse. You expect me to believe none of that bothers? I know different. I was there when you pulled up Clarence's drawers at Miss Rainey's house. So don't be acting to me like you don't care. It bothers. Plenty."

The war between me and Washington?

Too late I see it wasn't just me and the government boys, see how that fight spilled over, leaked elsewhere, causing family feuds in a Sunday kitchen that should have been host to milk belches and nothing but. And I regret it, I do. But the dead can't go back and live over. All we're allowed is seeing clearer where we erred. In that moment I had no notion of housebound ruckus. Under a bowl of blue sky, mourning doves mourning in the brush, I was pondering what a man touched in the head does to top showing off his privates in public.

Irene, finally herded to the door, swings round for one last stinger.

"You think you can take care of everything because you're the boy, but you can't. You're still a young'un, no matter how tall."

"Thanks for the clarification. Next time I want your opinion, I'll take a number."

"Lucian?"

"She's gone, Mama."

But just to make sure Irene doesn't circle back, he watches that Buick's tail fin slice air for a country mile.

Dead, you understand love better. Look forward to that.

Harrison

No practicing for commencement allowed on Sunday, so gym's deserted, school's deserted, schoolyard deserted, just me and the Firebird parked on the lip of the baseball field, waiting for later.

Can't start now, not yet, not till it's dark. Darker, anyhow. Get to the beach too soon and anyone might see me. Nell, Lucian, anyone.

Something spooky about a baseball diamond at twilight. Like any blink might reload the bases with white boys drooling Juicy Fruit, restart the inning, its torment. Mawatuck never had a baseball team worth shit—before integration, since. Basketball colored up but not baseball. Won't catch me squinting into the sun for balls than might never come. One slow fucking game: baseball.

"You expect white boys to know how to run? Why's that? No one's ever chasing THEM."

Jocelyn's take.

Lucian had a different rag.

"Don't be snickering at the lame white boys, Harrison. You'll wound tender Hornet morale."

Hard not to snicker when nobody on the team ever tried to catch a pop-up or put a glove to a grounder, most of them high from the same bag of weed that mellowed out the superintendent's son. Surrounded by a bunch of the worthless, Mitchell Sears still stood out. Swung the bat like a crippled girl, dropped balls that hadn't even been thrown. And there to take in every failure: Superintendent/Daddy Maynard Sears, minus the tie and jacket, white shirtsleeves rolled past the elbow, face pressed against mesh fence, calling out pointers: "Choke up, Mitchie. Choke up." Other team steady hoochey-cooing the blond boy with hair that wouldn't stay shoved beneath his cap.

Trade places with Mitchell Sears? Another one of those supposed-to-be white princes?

Un-a, man.

No *thanks*.

Even before Donnie Anderson clamped on the handcuffs and dragged the poor fuck off to Mawatuck jail, nobody was hot to be that son of. Mitchell Sears could shit white and be no one to envy.

Gym's probably unlocked, always is, commencement prep or none. Nothing stopping me from throwing some hoops, free throws, lay-ups, jumpers, aiming for the swish or the bank shot, letting the ball bounce and roll, no other hands grabbing, no other eyes watching. Me playing me. Classrooms probably open too. Founding fucking fathers of Mawatuck High never dreamed feet darker than the floorboards would be padding up and down the hallways, black kids graduating alongside their recognized kin. And if they had? Dreamed it? Never would have hammered in the first nail, most likely. Better farm kids grow up ignorant than "sullied," mingling with my color and shades of.

Stand at the south end of the hallway, whistle or scream, echo rolls out like a yoyo on endless string.

My locker, Jocelyn's locker, Mrs. Avery's homeroom, all on the south end.

A conspiracy, according to Jocelyn.

"Bunching everything black. Trying to keep us in one place, OUR place."

Except Lucian's locker is next to mine, Nell's not too far down, and both of them lily white.

Jocelyn ever found out I trailed them to the beach—Lucian, Nell, Jimmy Barnard, those other two white bitches—my ass would come in for nonstop abuse, man. Nothing worse in Jocelyn's Book of Wrong than attempting to "blend." But a person can be curious, check out the other side without defecting—whatever Jocelyn says.

Long as I take it slow, schoolyard to Barco, it'll be okay, full dark or near it by the time I get to The Lido. Just gotta take it slow. Lucian beside me, he'd be saying, "God Almighty, what's the world coming to? Firebird taking it slow?" But the Fairlaine's the one got ticketed, pulled over at the Aydlett turnoff, speed trap set up behind a bunch of pyracantha.

"See what happens when the county hires too many cops?" Lucian jawed then, sounding like his daddy. "Nothing else to do but give out tickets."

Didn't get a fucking ticket the day the Broomstick sent us begging yearbook ads. Crept along this fucking highway, none of us eager to do that bidding. White-owned businesses, Nell and Lucian took turns, slinking in. Black barbershops, vegetable stands, this boy entered, hand extended. Lucian and Nell never got a dime but everybody I asked dug into the change box, wanting to support "the integrated school."

Couldn't have that kind of sacrifice on my conscience, man.

"You ain't getting me out of this car again," I said.

And Nell chimed in: "Me either."

And Lucian said: "Thank God Almighty. But we ain't heading back to school. Not holding three signed excuses to stay the fuck out."

Kept on riding just to be riding, back roads, short cuts.

"Remember that house game of yours, Amelia Nell?" Lucian said and got himself an argument.

"*Mine*? You invented it."

"The hell you say. Back me up, Harrison."

Like I knew what the fuck they were talking about.

Like I was *there*.

"We used to take turns, picking out houses. If we called them, they were ours," Nell tried to explain.

A white kids' game if ever there was.

White white white.

"Amelia Nell always had to have the Wrights' house. Threw a hissy fit otherwise."

"And Loo-shun always had to have that one with the magnolias at Harbor Point."

"You bet. Why settle for a house when you can have yourself a plantation with all the trimmings?"

Got that much out before his neck flushed and Nell started rocking in misery between us.

"Sorry, Harrison. That came out...wrong."

Like I'd accused him of pining for a mammy.

"Sorry about what, man? What you got to be sorry about?"

Thinking all the time *if I lived in a dump like you, Carter, I'd be wanting to trade up too.*

"I didn't mean..."

"Yeah, yeah, so why we still talking about it?"

"Lucian's right, though," Nell said, slipping toward a different kind of anxious. "If I didn't get the Wrights' house, I'd always get really upset."

"Why's that?" I asked and landed us in something worse than Confederate crap.

"I guess I thought something awful would happen at the beach. If I didn't get my pick."

And, just like that, Lucian's got more than offending me to worry about, one curve between us and the Sound, Mawatuck Bridge coming up fast, Mawatuck Bridge where something awful did happen. Lucian's quick where Nell's concerned but, shit. You can't travel this road and *not* see a bridge, not smell water. Ditches, creeks, canals, inlets, air heavy enough to drip, cloudy day or cloudless, and all that before you even get close to Sound white caps.

How'd Lucian ever get Nell to The Lido past so much water without her falling into funk? Rib her about dancing? Claim Jimmy Barnard couldn't wait to give her a hickey?

Shit like that, maybe.

Stupid shit like that.

Squashed and squatty's how The Lido looks. Like maybe a hurricane tore off part of the second floor and someone slapped a roof on what was left. But Lucian says squatty's how it was built. Ceilings low enough to scrape a tall boy's head, he says. Management skimped on the window work too. You can see that much from the outside. No glass, not even screens. Just squared off wall holes for ventilation, but holes that let the music through. Long as the ocean's calm, no wind whipping up the surf, you can hear every lick of "Be Young, Be Foolish, Be Happy" from the dunes. Don't even need to be inside.

Sky's finally gone dark enough for Lido lights to shine. Nobody's gonna notice black Harrison's blue Firebird on the drive by. Safe now. Safe as it can be.

Bouncer/basher Leroy on guard next to the entrance. Muscle shirt to show off his anchor tattoos, arms crossed but fingers twitchy, waiting for someone to burp wrong.

Boss's "primary ugly," Lucian calls Leroy.

"It's like word went out. Look like a ape? Grunt like a ape? Okay then, you're hired."

Nell hates Leroy. Lucian too, he just doesn't advertise the fact. Can't be too cautious where Leroy's concerned. Threw a general's son from Virginia out one of those screen-less windows last summer. Car hood broke the pitched out's fall, but the general sued regardless, expecting justice for his neck-braced son in Boss's terrain.

Uh-huh.

Like giving air money, those wasted lawyer fees.

But Boss let loose some cash too, Lucian said. Greased plenty of palms to make double sure the verdict went his way. On the stand, Leroy testified he was "just doing his job" besides which he "didn't break skin." About to get worked up all over again when the judge ordered a recess. Hour later, no harm/no foul verdict and that was that.

Except Boss pulled Leroy off bouncer duty for a week.

Extra precaution.

"Like that did anyone a favor," Nell grumped.

"Just mixed bitter with mean," Lucian agreed. "Never a good thing, Leroy bitter-mean."

On show tonight, that pairing. Soon as a skinny white boy drops a candy wrapper too close to Leroy's nose, Leroy's got him twirled like a baton, teeth slammed next to that litter. Victim chewing grit and plastic along with chocolate. Acting like it's his favorite meal. Favorite dining position.

Thank you, Mr. Leroy! Thank you, sir!

Lucian parked near the back of the lot tonight, Jimmy Barnard's beater truck alongside the Fairlaine. Allison's mama's canary-colored Corvair nearby. Inside, all of them must be, beyond the scope of Leroy's watchtower.

Maybe Lucian said, in passing: "Evening, Leroy."

Maybe Leroy didn't so much as grunt.

Maybe Nell said: "Friend-ly." Made a face. Started to back-sass before Lucian yanked her along.

Maybe Jimmy Barnard, jiggling on one foot, yipped: "Hey, Leroy, hey man, packing some fine merchandise tonight, extra fine, brought in last weekend. Free samples, man. You wanna test hit?"

Leroy maybe thinking *I want a free hit, I don't need no invitation, runt.*

Just behind those double screen entrance doors, to the left, there's a soda fountain, Lucian said.

Orange crush, malts, burgers, french fries. Banana splits.

"Grease pit," Nell pooh-poohed. "How long you think that oil's been in the deep fryer? A century?"

Asking Lucian, not me.

Past the soda fountain, against the back wall: three pool tables, Jimmy and gang's check-in spot.

"If only they'd *stay* downstairs," Nell said, that comment to anyone who'd listen.

"You know what used to be in there, Harrison?"

Mama asking, in her lesson voice, long ago.

"A bowling alley. Not an automated system. Another kind of labor."

Slave labor she could have said and been done with it. But no, she had to draw out the story: black men playing fetch, rushing between lanes, righting fallen pins, nothing but knees and thighs and set-up hands to the white bowlers they served. White customers irritated by any delay, thinking *shiftless niggers. Look at 'em, taking their own sweet time.*

"And you know how much those men were paid, Harrison? On their feet, running, all day long? *Fifty cents.*"

Going rate for black phantoms, huh? Fifty cents a day.

"Boss is SUCH a cheap bastard," Nell griped. "Wouldn't you think he'd at last paint over the *alley numbers*?"

Second-guessing the whys and how of a slimy white businessman—not exactly a black boy adventure.

"How much you guess Boss pays his second-floor cashier, Amelia Nell? Might be a job for you: snatching people's money, planting that purple stamp on every wrist."

Not *every* wrist, I could have said. Not *every* wrist of *every* color.

"Freckles the size of marbles. Mouthful of gold teeth, rooster wattle for a neck. Yeah, Amelia Nell, I do believe you could give that gal a run for Boss's beauty spot."

Got bopped hard for that tease, deserved it too. But the reason Lucian told the tale he told was me. For my benefit. On my account. He and Nell were *there. They* didn't need reminding.

"See, Harrison, when Leroy's not bashing heads, Boss keeps him busy bussing beer cans, circling round with a garbage can tucked under his armpit. So one night Miss Amelia Nell here makes the mistake of looking elsewhere..."

"*I* didn't make the mistake. *He* did."

"Uh-huh. Anyway, Harrison, listen. Leroy reaches out his paw, swipes the table clear, moves along. But what does he hear behind him? This one screaming: 'Hey, you! HEY YOU!'"

Lucian half talking, half giggling.

"I mean, taking on Leroy. Amelia Nell. About half the size of the man's knuckle! You gotta picture it, Harrison. Leroy, swerving round, every muscle puffed up. 'You calling ME?' And Amelia Nell, fearless as piss: 'Yeah, I'm calling you. That beer you snatched? I wasn't finished with it.'"

Lucian laughing so hard by then he has to stop to wipe his eyes.

"So Leroy, Leroy's stunned, man. Leroy's AMAZED. Contradicted AND contradicted by a shrimpboat girlie. So, so, listen, so after he's done staring, jaw on the floor, after he's gulped and stuttered a few times, the best, the very best, Leroy can come up with is: 'Was too finished.' WAS TOO FINISHED! Wait, wait, it gets better. Amelia Nell, she's learned nothing in the last sixty seconds either, Leroy snorting like a bull close range, and she says, she says: 'WAS NOT!'"

"Enjoying yourself a little too much at my expense, aren't you, sport?"

But Nell's giggling too. Impossible not to, watching Lucian bust a gut.

"So what happened then?"

Because I could picture it: Nell climbing on to a beer-soaked bench, hectoring Leroy, Leroy holding back, but just, from using her skinny butt for a game of bouncer ball.

"Yeah, Loo-shun. Keep going. Tell Harrison what you did then, you spineless coward."

"Whew" is all Lucian manages.

"You tell, Nell."

"Rat him out?"

Lucian lifts his arm like: *be my guest.*

"Come on. Lucian might never catch his breath again."

"Okay. I'll tell. This big boy, here? This big baby squeaks: 'Not a problem, Leroy, not a problem. Girl needed a fresh brew anyhow.' Then tears off to buy another beer because a dumb shit can't tell full from empty."

"I did that. Do it again. Happy to give in to bouncer Leroy."

"Except I didn't WANT Leroy given in to."

"Didn't want to, but should have. In a jiff."

"Why's that?"

"Why's THAT, Amelia Nell? God Almighty!"

"God Almighty yourself. If people didn't give in to that goon..."

"They'd be dead."

Oops. Wrong word. Both pouting now.

"Somebody had to show some belly and fast. You were closing in on serious hurt, girl."

Censored version—I could tell. Somewhere inside Lucian's head, a rougher, cruder comeback playing. Something to the tune of *you imagine Leroy cares you got a hole between your legs? Just makes you a lighter toss.*

But even cleaned up/toned down that rebuke had effect.

Nell listens to Lucian. They might argue and tussle but in the end, when he gets that look he gets, like the world's one big stomp in a cesspool, it's her that gives in, not Lucian.

"I guess," she said that day, fingers picking at her mouth. "But...sometimes...sometimes The Lido really gives me the creeps."

"For good reason," Lucian said.

Wet fingers on my arm.

"See, Harrison. See all the fun you're missing?"

And what was I supposed to say to that?

Yippee?

Clarence

Briefly, briefly: Boss's enterprise, the one Harrison's staring at, mooning over like it's a rejecting girl? He's right. Not entirely on the up and up. Nobody on that payroll cares whether a customer's true eighteen or a little shy thereof. But that skirting the strict letter and limits of the law—that's Lido tradition. Boss the First ran the place same way, back when the beach road was still sand and planks. Uncle Travis, Leonard's daddy, my daddy's brother, used to tell how he and his buddies decided to take advantage of a ready market, sell some swamp sour to Boss the First. Only hitch: none of 'em knew nuthin' about building or operating a still. Good swamp whiskey, and it's a category all its own, takes a steady hand. Wildcatter's got to do more than put on hip boots, slog through a vine maze and restrain himself from guzzling the profits. First and foremost, he's got to keep from blowing himself up. Takes patience and cunning to prosper from a whiskey still—so naturally Uncle Travis and cronies gave it up.

All my days, people mistook me for Uncle Travis's feckless son.

Boss the Second, the gentleman Harrison hasn't yet glimpsed, he's no pick of the litter, neck permanently kinked to one side, head heavy, proportion-wise. Left hand's missing some digits, those fingers caught jammed where they didn't belong. He does keep a healthy stack of bills in the backroom, this Boss does, primarily because he loves to count and fondle that green greasy. And so what, to that? Gazing into mirrors can't be a pleasure for the man. The muscle he employs gets a salary, plus bed and breakfast. Before Boss took them in, most of those boys and men wandered the streets north of Ocean Park, thrown off docked ships, spending the last of their Navy pay on skin ink. Boss gave them something to do and reason to do it. Ain't nothing wrong with those employment terms or with Boss for offering them.

Families come to be by all means of strange coincidence. Rescue too. If you were loyal to Boss the Second, he stayed loyal to you. Took some of that greasy green and bribed the necessary to keep Leroy from confinement, didn't he? No Man of the Year, this year or any, but people arguing for a Lido shutdown don't understand human nature, other kind of nature either. You cut out a patch of swamp something's going to sprout in that absence, fill in quick. Same with Boss's job. If he closed up tomorrow, there'd be a Lido Two opening next week because dancehalls turn a profit. Always have, always will.

Harrison

Black men can sing, strut, harmonize on Boss's stage but can't piss in his toilets. Plenty of times I've watched them hightail it down the backstairs after a set, unzipping along the way, can hardly wait to take a whiz.

Sequin jackets for stage dazzle, silver for the backup singers, red for the lead. Pompadours high and glistening.

Considered sneaking over to share a cig or weed, pump them for road stories, where they played in Myrtle Beach and farther south, who they prefer: Otis, Wilson, Smoky, Fats. Hang out with those lean, bored, sparkling music men till break time's end.

Maybe they'd say: "Come on up behind us. We'll get you in."

Maybe they'd say: "What you hanging around this whitewash for? Drive up to Bartock you want to hear get-down not watered down."

Maybe if I listened from the backstairs instead of the dunes, I'd be able to hear the mock in "You're Gonna Hate Yourself in the Mornin'," feel those lyrics cut both ways—at a pale crowd of shitty dancers, at darker brothers providing the beat.

Maybe.

Right now I'm picturing this second-floor action: Allison in full Vampira makeup, prancing over to Nell and Lucian's booth, demanding he partner up for the ballad in progress. On the dance floor already, Melinda draped over Jimmy Barnard like a coat on a coat rack, watching her pal's antics, watching with a grudge.

Lucian cocking an eyebrow, thinking *can Allison Ferrell be THIS dumb?*

Wide open, man, wide open for put-down.

"Surely you can slow dance!"

"Surely I can't."

"Then it's time to learn."

Through steady-on pester, Lucian thinking *damn if she ain't that dumb.*

"Do me a favor, Carter. Decide before the song ends."

But a favor's not exactly what Allison's in for.

"Pass."

"What?!"

"Pass—but feel free to come begging again."

"Fucker."

"Still gonna stick with that pass."

Allison hissing, Lucian giggling, when a rank stranger—from another school, another conference, maybe even a sand fiddler high school—dips in toward Nell.

"What about you? Would *you* like to dance?"

Handsome in that red/white boy way.

Maybe bearing the faintest resemblance to a superintendent's son.

Shocks the whole bunch, Lucian included, Nell accepting that stranger's hand, following him to a dancing spot.

"Get a load of THAT."

"Some fucking nerve."

"Why is she dancing with *him*?!?!"

But after a few false starts Nell and her new guy don't look half bad together, begin to sync up rhythms, generate some body heat, start to look almost like they were destined to dance duo at Boss's Lido.

"I thought she didn't like to dance."

"Changed her mind, I'd say, from the look of that clinch."

"Talk about sinking to the bottom of the barrel."

"Rock bottom."

"That guy's not even LOCAL, man!"

"She doesn't even *know* the guy!"

Which would be about all the Allison/Melinda/Jimmy, et cetera badmouthing Lucian would stomach before saying: "Is that the rule? You can only dance with someone you know?"

Over now, if any of it happened, because there's Lucian, bumping the entrance door with his ass to protect his lit cigarette, Nell half a step behind and stranger-less, the pair of them part flesh, part shadow beneath The Lido's yellow lights. Then Nell goes back inside and it's just Lucian in that bulb glow, taking in salt air, alone with his smoke till Leroy steps out.

On patrol but wising off. Muttering something like: "A girl that scrawny? Best go easy with that big cock of yours."

Lucian snarling: "Not my girlfriend, stud. Cousin."

Probably too fine a distinction for Leroy, half of Mawatuck too.

So maybe, instead, Lucian tries: "Anyone ever call you a common son of a bitch?"

Or: "Say that again and we'll see who's got a cock worth keeping."

Or...

Except Lucian's no fool and steers clear of playing one. That's his daddy's turf.

Wouldn't mind being a fly by Lucian's ear now, but that first visit from the feds, the one that started Clarence on his fool path? Too much in the thick of that thing.

IRS guys drove the blandest car imaginable. Tan Plymouth, nothing but basic chrome. Not a bit of stylin'. Office-white driver and passenger squirming out, impetigo smear the only way to tell those two apart.

Purply blue shows up bad on white skin—real bad.

Young enough for cowboys and Indians, me and Lucian, but not so young we didn't recognize trouble carrying briefcases. Any second expected *somebody* to send me home—Mrs. Carter, if not Clarence. Must have needed that order to scoot because without it there I stayed, scared as Lucian by the way his mama left her basket of damp laundry, walking from that clothesline like no chore behind her mattered quite so much as what she faced.

Lucian's daddy—different attitude entirely. Waltzed out of the house like he had all day to do it, hair wet from washing.

"Mr. Carter, my name is Felcher. This is Simmons."

Long, long speech after that about Mr. Carter's obligations, all the obligations Mr. Carter had ignored. Failure to respond to said letter, said date. Failure to respond to said follow-up letter, said follow-up date.

That kind of shit.

Since said U.S. citizen in 1968 lived without a telephone, no "recourse" but a surprise at-home visit to discuss unpaid taxes '63 to '65.

Clarence hee-hawed, danced in place.

"Who put you up to this, fellas? Tell the truth, now. Cousin Leonard? What's your best guess, Rosie? Leonard smart enough to think this one up by himself? Naw, naw. That scoundrel had some help. Had to."

During that net cast of wonder, IRS guys kept their mouths shut, eyes peeled. Then the infected one cleared his throat—not fighting phlegm, prepping for clash.

"Unpaid taxes are no laughing matter to the U.S. government, Mr. Carter. The U.S. government takes tax evaders very, very seriously."

Like how many times could he work in "U.S. Government"? Ready, set, GO!

Lucian latched onto his mama's skirts, too upset to care if I saw or didn't. Still clinging tight when the taxmen escorted his mama offside.

Only one unconcerned, the tax evader himself. Clarence wandered my way, squatted, winked.

"You boys ask nice, government fellas might ride ya'll around in that dirt-colored Plymouth."

Serious

Do you understand

Dangerous

Gravity
Talk
Explain
Husband
filtering through Clarence jabber.

One tan car advantage: shows less dust. When they drove off the first time, a grit mist followed, but not Clarence. Not the first time.

I could have leapt across the ditch, tore off for my house, nobody stopping me or trying to, but still I stayed like someone mesmerized by accident, accident on the verge. Lucian's mama weeping, Lucian tuning up to join her and Clarence, Clarence acting like someone pulled one plug, stuck in another—ranting, raving, going for his fucking shotgun, giggles a thing of the past, man. "Holy Jesus," I must have muttered a hundred times, spine pressed tight against clapboard, hands over my eyes, not even tempted to peek during that return visit shooting spree.

"Daddy's not that bad a shot," Lucian ventured, years later, revisiting that history lesson. "I figure he was aiming for the radio antenna all along, don't you?"

Wanting that opinion seconded. Needing my agreement to back up that not-quite-solid belief.

Lucian's the son of a man doesn't know when to quit, but Lucian himself does. Whatever he said to Leroy and Leroy to him, they've parted company with neither one gashed or bleeding.

One more band set, one last beer call and this Lido night will be gone too. Mawatuck crew piling in their cars, heading home, down the road, across a bridge, moonshine on flat water, brightening up night currents. Lucian jiving fast and light to get Nell across that span. Allison and Melinda ignorant of the rev on that perky Corvair, wasting that engine's gift. Jimmy Barnard and his crowd higher than beer high, playing chicken over the rise. Clueless, all of them, who's been watching, following, taking it all in, man. Taking in what he can.

Once they clear out, once those yellow lights blink off, piece of cake to park up close under one of those windows. Leap from the Firebird's hood, grab hold of ledge, haul myself up and over for a little after-hours sightsee of their whites-only hive.

Dreaming, black boy. Nothing but.

Crashing waves, surf in churn, nothing drowns out Jocelyn-voice.

Goading.

Daring.

Bitch.

No way you're getting in there. Sand dune's close as you'll ever be.

One of these nights, we'll see how close, we'll see who's dreaming.

What's that, black boy? Promise or threat?

Clarence

Me and Harrison don't recall that government visit precisely the same. But he saw some things I missed. Dead, I can reposition. Share a hawk's view of Rosie rounding the house, wash forgotten, see how fast she understood that sedans packing suits counted for more than passing nuisance.

Even after I heard her calling, I didn't rush to dry off, button my shirt. Not hurrying was my first mistake. Second one was strolling out casual, taking in those uninvited guests and assuming my leg was being yanked but good.

But, listen: that black tie/black shoe get-up? Briefcases and hair lacquered to match? Came off as costume. Still does.

"'Fess up now," I said through a whinny-laugh. "Did Cousin Leonard send you? Is he the one set up this prank?"

Leonard considered himself a horseshoe champ, but I'd beat him three times running in front of his store buddies. So him conniving to get even, sending round that team of grimness, wasn't half far-fetched. Little elaborate for Leonard's usual paybacks, but that just made it seem all the funnier—for about a minute.

"The U.S. Government doesn't consider unpaid taxes a joke, Mr. Carter," the short one of the pair spouted, both of them serious as saw blades.

Highhandedness's got a brief life, comedy wise. Plenty of ways to settle opinion differences without uppityness entering the picture. Those whipping boys, if they'd come off reasonable, willing to indulge in some give and take, I suspect I'd have responded in kind, agreed to some system of paying off what they claimed I owed, month by month, week by week. But when the government roars up to my house, treats me like a tried and convicted thief, tries its best to scare the bejesus out of me and my family—un-a. Ask nice, maybe I'll roll over, throw up my legs, just to move things along. But act like I got no *choice* but to fall out trembling? Un-a, I say again. Not a Cracker anywhere'd agree to those surrender terms.

General rule, I wound down slow from amused. Enjoyed it too much to quit sooner. But that day the giggling halted early. Soon as they realized they weren't making any "progress with Mr. Carter," they crowded Rosie, whispering loud enough for me to hear: "You've got one hour, Mrs. Carter. Use it well."

Didn't care to share my hour's plans with those bully boys but when I tried with Rosie, she held up a hand, the other one working to pry Lucian off her skirts.

"You two boys go in the kitchen and cut yourselves some chocolate cake. Take care with the butcher knife. And eat it at the table. Harrison, hon? Can you help Lucian remember to stay in the kitchen, at the table?"

Lucian still tearful, Harrison terrified of every living adult right then, Rosie included.

"Yes'um," he said and took his pal by the hand.

Plymouth gone, boys gone too, but that hand of Rosie's constant pushing at the air between us.

"No, Clarence. Before you start in, you're going to listen to me."

Wasn't wild about listening then, ain't now. If I repeat all she said, I'll get cussing mad again, so this is the bunched-up version: governments are nothing to cross, governments don't give up, governments always, in the end, get what they're after. Got the time, the money, the resources, the manpower to do it. Will hassle a low-end tax evader till kingdom come. Didn't I understand no single man ever fought a cavalry and won?

Because I loved the woman I let her tear through that speech without too many interruptions but none of what she argued changed my mind. When that car the color of kid turd returned, Clarence Carter and a shotgun said hi.

Never aimed higher than rubber tires but got their attention regardless. Second trip, they stayed inside their vehicle, engine running loud and ragged on dirty sparks. Rosie screaming, Lucian bawling, only quiet one in the bunch was Harrison, brown mouth chocolate smeared, just his bad luck to get caught in the middle of a white man's skirmish.

"You're making a mistake, Mr. Carter!"

"A very serious mistake!"

Nothing wrong with my windpipe. I could holler loud as them.

"You got to the count of three to back that jalopy elsewhere."

"Are you *threatening* an agent of the federal government, Mr. Carter?"

"One," I said.

"Two," I said, and Rosie flew at me, trying to wrestle the gun away.

"Three," I said, and Lucian picked up a handful of oyster shells and started pelting their fender, Harrison skittering backwards fast as his talent would allow.

"We'll be back, Mr. Carter," the partner of shorty yelled. "And next time we won't be so understanding."

So, see, it wasn't just me upping the ante. They flung out their own set of threats before leaving me with a woman a little too Lily-like in her stare and glare.

"Clarence Carter, do you have any idea what you just started?"

Can't claim I altogether did. But pretty soon I came around to believing what my Rosie said about a lone shotgun. To keep those rascals and the power they served at bay, Clarence Carter was going to need a sneakier weapon than a cocked firearm.

Mabel

First thought, first come to on that room-for-nothing sofa: it's Amelia hovering, dragging her hair in my eyes. Then I take a breath, smell those strands have been stewing in their own juices awhile and know it can't be Amelia. Amelia's hair never lost the smell of soap and blossom, scalp grease never allowed to thrive on that head, the girl too fond of bounce and curl, bounce and curl.

It's Amelia's young'un bending overly close.

"Mabel? Mabel? Can you hear me? Can you talk?"

Certainly I can hear and speak. Just not inclined to do either at the moment. Still pondering Amelia, wondering if when my time does come we'll recognize each other, she stuck at 20, me lasting long enough to be her grandma too.

"Mabel? Can you sit up? Do you want some water? How about a glass of tea, lots of ice?"

Nattering young'un. Always nattering. Her mama laughed more, talked less, had her secrets, kept them. Amelia wouldn't look half so worried, hanging over me. She'd assume whatever ailed would pass. No sense in making a production. No sense in the fret. And here crouches her child, gnawing on her fingernails, so scared her fear's beginning to outstink greasy hair.

But what do I see, soon as that grease curtain shifts? A sure-fire vision of Enon Halston's stand-in, cut up with concern, wringing his hands while Amelia Nell chews hers.

"Get gone, Satan," I say and hear: "See, she's talking now. She's answering."

Vision's got the voice of Enon too. Down to the curly whine always twists a statement's end.

Devil having fun with Mabel Stallings before she's even dead.

Except Amelia Nell's talking to that vision too, telling him to back back, step away. Confirmation that varmint's real and in my living room.

"What you thinking, young'un, letting a Halston sneak in here?"

"You were out COLD, Mabel! I had to get you in. Out of the heat."

"Could have made a tent with a blanket."

"You PASSED OUT, Mabel! I was frantic."

Waking up to a Halston don't calm this heart none either.

Rest of the afternoon, what do I have to put up with but Amelia Nell soaking me with washcloths, training two electric fans at my head, both of them switched high.

Watered and breezed, this old woman, watered and breezed.

"Thought you had plans this evening."

"The Lido, you mean? That was before."

"Before what? Your grandma had a little dizzy spell?"

"A LITTLE dizzy spell?"

"Which she's recovered from. You want to make me feel even better, go off and leave me free of your tending."

Urging the same trip her mama never came back from, but I can't let that kind of fussing over me go on and on. Come the time when I might need her to play nursemaid. No need practicing beforehand.

"You heard me. Go on. Get ready. And wash that hair."

Reluctant, reluctant.

Peeking around the bathroom door in nothing but a towel, checking to see if I'm still conscious.

"Concentrate on that hair! Your grandma's fine."

Head aching something fierce, but otherwise fine.

Lucian Carter never has learned to take that driveway turn without showering my hydrangeas with dust. Imagine I'm rid of the both of them, but no, here they come, trooping back.

"How about we stick around, Cousin Mabel?" Clarence's son suggests. "Keep you entertained."

"Nothing doing. Git."

"Didn't I tell you?"

"Better hear what you're turning down first. Poker tricks, half a dozen if one."

"You two ain't in that car and moving before I get to the sink we'll see whose afternoon turns out worse."

"Argues good as new," Lucian says.

"And who's causing me to keep at it? Git, I say."

I see them from the window, both of them grave as onions, climbing into that Ford like it's a punishment. My Amelia would have been halfway to the beach by now and thrilled about it.

Sometimes I believe the Lord gave me one kind of young'un and when I messed up that guardianship, gave me the opposite to test if I'd mess up just as bad, second time.

In the car. In their seats. Car starts, but doesn't move an inch. Gabbing, gabbing, until the engine shuts off. Then out they pile again, tacking in my direction till I cut them off at the screen door.

"What you left? Money? Keys?"

Daring either to say *left an old puny woman, that's what.*

"It's Sunday. Nothing happening at The Lido anyway."

"Come on, Mabel. Let us back in."

"Not going to happen, Missy."

"We don't have to play cards, if that's what you're dreading. Lucian does magic tricks too."

"I do, indeed. What's your pleasure, Cousin Mabel? Disappearing rabbits, quarters plucked from your ear?"

Don't Clarence Carter's son wish he did know a few magic spells? Come in mighty handy.

And after such nonsense talk there it sputters: next generation Clarence giggle, infecting Amelia Nell.

Whatever happens, they left here laughing—that's what I keep telling myself, Sunday evening rolling toward Monday, clock ticking, me in this damn rocking chair, watching for car lights to silver up hydrangea, streak this room in ribbons of white. Old nervous woman who should have been in bed long ago, waiting up, waiting to make sure this overheated night the Stallings left to her has crossed Sound to ocean and back again on a bridge that did what a bridge is supposed to do: keep her grandyoung'un safe, keep my Amelia Nell from breathing water.

Harrison

Monday mornings, always the same. Four years of coming round that gym corner, running up against a wall of white boys puffing like it's their last prayer. And every time this black boy's balls draw up in a pinch.

Numb nuts. Numb nuts Doxey.

And that's *expecting* to see a crew of pale huddled before first bell.

Taken by surprise...can't even fathom, man.

"Prancing round that corner, wearing your Uncle Tom/Stepin Fetchit grin. Straining so hard to please."

Jocelyn's wrong there—not a grinning situation, trying to scope a free spot, settle, horn in on no one else's wall space but still claim my own.

Alternative is—what? Pretend there's no official outdoor smoking lounge at Mawatuck High? Start a rival, blacks-only smoking club around the next corner?

Un-a.

If this is where Mawatuck males smoke, here's where this Mawatuck male's going to do his smoking.

Girls, black or white. Forget it. They've got bathroom stalls to light up in, stub flush, finish off with breath mints and gargle to disguise the scent of cig. Not welcome here, not invited.

Donnie Anderson's not on the invitation list either, man, but he showed up all the same. Showed up, charged in, got a chokehold on yellow-haired Mitchell Sears, yellow windbreaker bulging with stash, superintendent daddy next building over no help to the perp at all.

After that law raid even dimwit Jimmy Barnard took his dealing to the cornfield, off school property proper.

Sheriff's deputy barges in, everyone's jumpy, but the first day I come around, Jimmy stiffens up like someone just shoved a rod up his ass, the rest of that tight, closed pack going still and silent as stone.

Whatever Jocelyn THINKS she knows about me, I didn't turn tail, even before Lucian sidestepped to get between me and them, relit his own dead Marlboro, offered me a fresh one, forcing Jimmy and crew to burn ash too, playact it was no biggie, me there or not.

Bullshit to that.

Every inch of Jimmy Barnard resented my presence and showed it: chin, spine, even the balls of his fucking feet. Four years later, if he thought he could get away with it, he'd still call me a coon to my face.

But I'll say this for Jimmy Barnard: he's a bigot with range, black's not the only thing he hates. Mitchell Sears passed his color test, but everything else about the superintendent's son twisted Jimmy's jock. Son of privilege. Bigshot daddy. New kid on the block. Mountain twang that turned *ice* into *eyesss*—as in 'Eyesss tea, puhlease." Hillbilly, hippie, queer.

Except the hillbilly hippie queer son of privilege had it bad for Nell Stallings and she for him.

"I do believe Amelia Nell's all hot and bothered over a certain new ponytail."

Lucian got bopped hard for that one and no play to the belting, either.

"Fuck you, Lucian."

"Not my fucking we're discussing," Lucian said and ducked as quick as a big boy can.

Maybe Nell and Mitchell got around to doing more than batting eyelashes and looking stricken in the other's company before he got hauled off—maybe not. Skittish, both of them, afraid to show preference, afraid of hurt before it arrived. Standing side by side they looked like famine twins—if famine victims were ever white. Different fight styles, though. Nell brawls like a swamp cock, feathers flying. Mitchell Sears fought the way he swung a bat—downright pitiful.

The second or third time he came loping around the corner to join us smokers, he got ambushed by Jimmy's crowd, shoved to the ground and kept there by knees grinding his kidneys.

"Time for shearing, queer," Jimmy yelled and flipped open his pocketknife, Mitchell thrashing about like he could save Lancelot curls with squirm.

If Jimmy'd spent less time announcing, more time doing, a sizeable chunk of blond would have been gone before Lucian arrived, knocked Jimmy sideways and yanked Mitchell to his feet.

"What the fuck?!?!" Jimmy screeched, stomping like his playtime had been interrupted.

"You consider that head of yours a SHOWPIECE?"

Meaning Jimmy's larded up, slicked back greaser do.

To make sure that perfection hadn't been harmed, Jimmy reached up for a quick swipe and stroke. Big boo-boo. That pack of rats he calls pals started pointing, hooting, calling him a girlie girl.

What's a black boy to do in situations such? Watch, laugh along, take care not to laugh loudest or longest? Aim for the fill-in snigger-honk, safest bet. Because hunters of flowing blond can turn into hunters of kink, Lucian on your side or not.

"Asshole," Mitchell said, once he caught his breath. Able to say that from Lucian's shadow.

Then—big nothing. Lucian lighting up, Mitchell, fingers trembling, sucking at filtered nicotine like it was seedy weed, Jimmy doing the same, hood, hippie, giant and black boy all in a lump, inhaling legal till first bell.

Jocelyn says: "You think just because you played together naked as kids, Lucian's your grown-up buddy? LOYAL to the end? White sticks up for white, first, last and always."

But I went on that jailhouse pilgrimage too.

Mitchell Sears never acted less than friendly toward me, plus he was locked up, locked in without a key, on his way to a mid-state prison, the cause of his daddy's speedy resignation and in for God knows what kind of payback from that quarter.

Field niggers bussed from Florida had it better, man.

Entire drive to Mawatuck prison, Nell and Lucian bickered. As kids they used to rollerskate on a nearby airstrip, concrete rivered with cracks, Lucian claimed, Nell just as steady denying.

"Skating within sight of those guard towers? No way!"

"Yeah, we did. Lots. First you'd pretend the guards weren't there, then you'd complain every rifle was pointed straight at you and your skating went all to hell."

"NO WAY, I SAID!"

On and on, on and on.

In the gravel parking lot, Lucian cut the engine. Official visiting hour. Prison yard full of state-issue denim worn by desperate, sorrowful men. Through the chain-link fence they stared at us. Through the windshield we stared at them.

Since none of us knew how to dress for a prison visit, we overdid. Lucian and me in clean khakis, Nell in some kind of flowered skirt that clashed with the bouquet she was clutching. Riding in the backseat, one of Rose Carter's prize chocolate cakes.

Lined up at the gate for frisking, the three of us, stared at by guards and cons alike, whole bunch wondering *what's that black one doing with those other two? What's he tagging along for? What's his bid-ness? Why's he free to come and go?*

And who'd those big-gutted white guards pat down first?

Uh-huh.

Lucian next, but Nell they left alone.

"Hey! What about me?"

"I believe you're clean, sister," the guard said.

Shit.

Even a toy knife would have stuck out on that body, anywhere she tried to stash it.

"Who's he calling 'sister'?"

But Lucian had other problems to handle just then. Without so much as a please or thank you, Rose Carter's chocolate cake got filched.

"Need to check it out, son. You understand."

About understanding, Lucian didn't say one way or the other.

"He can't just take our cake!"

"Can. Did. There's Mitchell," Lucian said, shoving Nell along.

Easy to pick out in that crowd: a long-haired blond boy, escape risk—zip.

Entire history of Mawatuck jail, one breakout, total. Story was: inmate called for help, middle of the night, pain in his gut, hurting bad. Guard stepped in his cell to investigate and bam! Knocked cold. Convict didn't kill his jailor, didn't try, just stripped that uniform of cash and took off toward swamp.

Lock your doors and windows! Lock your cars!

Mama ransacked the dresser drawers, searching for a house key we'd never used before, never used since. Daddy started spending his nights on the back porch, scanning the woods line, pretending the entertainment was fireflies.

Concocting a cover story, but fearing what?

That a black man on the run might seek another black man's aid?

That a black man on the run might savage black before white?

Sheriff formed a stake-out search party around the edges of the swamp, private citizens happy to go sleepless for the chance to play vigilantes, bring in a con.

White search party. White vigilantes. Bored and restless, armed with guns and readymade excuses. What black man with minimal sense would volunteer to share that night post?

After a week had passed, no capture, no viper-fanged corpse either, Mama asked: "How long can a man survive a summer swamp, Furillo?"

"Already dead is my guess," Daddy said and must have believed because he canceled his porch watch.

I like to believe otherwise.

I like to believe that inmate tricked a guard, tricked the swamp, got away from both with just a few briar scratches and a white man's billfold. That's what I like to believe.

But Mitchell the wimp, man. Not only didn't look *capable* of scaling that voltage fence, didn't act *inclined*. Pleased to be there. Delighted. Relieved.

"Three squares a day and no Maynard! It's fucking heaven. One big vacation."

Fast chattering like he'd substituted speed for weed.

Out of courtesy Lucian grunted. I followed suit. But Nell's pouty frown got poutier.

"And guess what else? They've got a baseball team here. Can you believe it? Every Sunday we play the Albemarle inmates. And lemme tell you, *criminals* are a fucking sight *tougher* than Mawatuck Hornets. That guy over there?"

Actually pointed, risking all our lives.

"Know what he does before breakfast? Too hundred fingertip pushups. Two *hundred*."

Lucian's grunt that go-around was less forced. Mine too. We each sneaked a second peek at the finger athlete.

"Too bad I can't give you a tour of my room. Flea-infested mattress. My very own no-lid toilet."

"Stop it, Mitchell," Nell snapped.

"Stop what?" Blinking wide.

"You know what. This...grandstanding. This cock a doodle do bullshit. You're in PRISON, charged with felony possession."

"I'll never be hired for a government desk job. So what?"

"Tad more to it than that, Mitch," Lucian said.

"What's with these two, Harrison? So serious. So fucking DOWN."

"With good reason," I wanted to say. "Look around, dickbrain. This ain't no motel you've checked into."

Didn't say it, didn't have to, ample proof lumbering our way, big smile above bigger paunch, the return of what remained of Lucian's mama's chocolate cake. With a little bow the guard set that mangled confection next to Mitchell's jumpy thigh. Five "searching for a shiv" holes split apart the layers. Several servings disposed of in the name of safety as well.

"Huh," I believe is what Lucian remarked.

"Couldn't resist," the guard said, smacking his lips. "You be sure to tell the cook it was mighty good."

"I'll do that," Lucian replied, flat-eyed.

But Nell—what are you going to do about Nell? Girl needs to learn something between hanging back, cringing like a titmouse and charging like a fucking pit bull.

"Stinking son of a bitch, stinking big ass son of a bitch!" Hands riding high on those no-hip hips, watching the guard's sassy retreat.

Pistol strapped high, the slandered not a bit peeved by that girlie protest.

"Nell, Nell!"

Mitchell snatching at her arm, trying to turn her back toward him. "Know what the best part is? I'll never have to worry about being drafted. Even if Martians invade Mawatuck, I'm off the hook."

"Why did he do that?" she asked me, then Lucian. "To prove he could? To walk back here wearing that shit-eating grin?"

"Let it go, Amelia Nell. Nothing you can do, so let it go."

But Lucian said it bitter, bile bitter.

"Here, Nell, here," Mitchell yipped, and we all turned to see him trying to cut Rose Carter's finest cake with the dull knife of his finger, smearing chocolate all over himself. "See, look. It doesn't matter. Plenty left to go around. More than plenty."

Like some white boy in a minstrel show, blackface applied in chocolate. Chattering, posing.

Who'd ever want to switch places with Mitchell Sears? In jail or free?

Up shit crick paddleless, man. Tide heading out.

Clarence

Just need to slip in here a minute with some clarification.

First: Lucian breaking up fights behind the gym and saving the superintendent's son from a shearing—never knew a thing about either one of those flareups, neither one ever mentioned at our house. But Lucian's always been one, even as a big little boy, to think size obligated him to stick up for the pipsqueaks, not to earn gratitude or play the hero, nothing like that. More as a practical matter, bigger standing a better chance of getting the job done in a rumble. Every season, football coach tried to convince Lucian to play tackle—a position he'd have been good at, I suspect. But Lucian wasn't much interested in team sports. Too much team to them.

Second off: that convict Harrison referenced?

Didn't make it to the state line or even out of the swamp. Climbed a tree, survived the night, but jailor's cash couldn't buy him a meal in the middle of the Dismal. Hungrier he got, the more he thought moccasins were his friends. Had some snake handlers for kin, it must be said. Died with venom in his blood. Died desperate, yes, but not the least bit sorrowful. If the search party hadn't been chomping so loud on goodies the sheriff's wife brought round, they've have heard that life-finished soul sing his praise of open air, honor the chance to piss in peat moss.

Harrison

"Hey, bud, whacha pondering? Looking mighty serious this early hour."

Lucian, bumping my elbow.

Proof I've been separated from the here and now too long, over snacking on past happenings.

"Five days is what I'm pondering."

Stick up a palm, do a lazy finger countdown to support that lie.

"Five short ones till me and this schoolyard part company. For-ev-er."

"That's smiling news, son."

"Uh-huh. And this is my free-at-last, free-at-last, thank God Almighty, I'm free-at-last grin."

"I see, I see."

Give him half a chance, Lucian's happy to trade bullshit all day and half the night.

"My mistake, bud. Thought maybe you were feeling all choked up over our Jenny's rousing speech. *Reach out. Embrace the future. Give it a big ole bear hug.* Tore Jimmy up but good. Tell the folks, Jim-Jim. How you broke out bawling in your folding chair, taking all those valedictorian instructions to heart."

"Fuck if that's so. I didn't listen to the cunt."

"Yeah, Lord," Lucian keeps ribbing, louder than the bell. "Jimbo weeping, wailing, carrying on something fierce. Ya'll pretending nobody heard that godforsaken racket but me?"

"Eat puke, Carter," Jimmy says, then skitters off like the rodent he is.

Lucian drops his stub, laughs, having fun while he can because what's he got to look forward to? A diploma won't change his situation.

He'll still be living in Mawatuck, sleeping in his daddy's house because if he left, how would his mama manage?

No joke or all joke—that's what the future is to Lucian. Nothing else it can be.

Mrs. Avery's class, whole hour, set aside to review for tomorrow's exam. Jenny Lucas scribbling like a mad thing, straining forward in her seat, writing down every syllable, notebook filled to the margins and still petrified she'll miss something she already knows.

Valedictorian behavior.

The rest of us, we're gliding. Half asleep, half dreaming, full-on dreaming. Lucian crammed into his kiddie desk, eyes closed, Nell gnawing eraser instead of cuticles, Allison and Melinda per usual tittering, Jocelyn per usual glaring like she's personally acquainted with sticks smarter than Allison Ferrell and Melinda Larson.

But those white girls don't care with Jocelyn thinks or doesn't. Couldn't care less if she glares, growls or lights herself afire. Just don't care.

Soon as Mrs. Avery turns to face board, Allison turns to face Lucian.

Clucks at him till he opens one eye.

"I just want to say how sorry I am about your daddy and all."

"Sorry?"

"Uh-huh."

"*You're* sorry about *my* daddy."

Slows her down, that repeat, but doesn't shut her up. Nothing can—for long.

"That's right. Sorry about him scaring Miss Rainey and being naked in public and all."

Melinda tilts in Lucian's direction, plainly wishing she'd thought to offer comfort and consolation before Allison jumped in. Best be glad she didn't.

Best be very glad.

"Old news," Lucian says, his last tolerance.

"Still—it must be *such* a trial for your mama and yourself."

That does it.

"Well, thank you ever so kindly, Miss Allison. I'm ever so touched by your heartfelt concern. I'm sure my dear mama will be too, soon as I rush home to tell her."

"Cocksucker."

"Born and bred," Lucian says. "Next time you decide to strike up a chat, remember that."

All the while, Mrs. Avery's steady chalking numbers, textbook clutched in the crook of her arm like she's afraid to get too far from it, maybe wishing like us this school year was over, more than ready to be finished with a job Miss Ticson started. Mrs. Avery weighs in at about half Miss Ticson's poundage—even before Miss Ticson gave up wearing anything with a waist. Last few weeks before Miss Ticson took off to deliver a "nephew" in Florida, she resembled a milk cow, wide and low-slung. But tiny can be too tiny, tidy too tidy. Every seam of Mrs. Avery's dress ironed flat, every curl on her head twisted tight. In a classroom, a little heft, a little wild-eye, works to a teacher's advantage.

"Mrs. Avery?"

Allison again.

"The de-ri-va-tion of log-a-rith-ms?"

"Yes?"

"I don't understand how, they're, uh, dee-rived."

"Since when have you understood anything, air pocket?"

Jimmy Barnard, of all people, asking. Still that snipe gets widespread approval. Nods all around.

"Well we're SUPPOSED to understand! Miss Ticson explained it."

"God Almighty, here we go," Lucian groans.

"What the fuck do you care?"

Damn good question, whoever shouted it. The minute Mrs. Avery launches into an explanation complicated enough to panic Jenny Lucas, Allison starts bouncing up and down in her seat, whispering to Melinda.

Nell holds up her trig book, points at a chart of derived logarithms. "Forgot how to flip pages? Try licking your thumb."

Jocelyn McPherson just taking it all in, steady taking it in.

"Does that help?" Mrs. Avery asks finally, mercifully, laying aside squeaky chalk.

"Not really."

"Which part are you having trouble understanding?" Still trying to teach, not yet wise to the put-on.

Spotlight square on her, the twat's in no hurry to answer. Fingers in her hair, twisting.

"Allison? Which part are you confused by?"

"Well...EVERYTHING, the way you say it."

Butt slapped, Mrs. Avery couldn't look more flustered.

Cross flaming in her face, Jocelyn McPherson couldn't look readier to attack.

Because what Allison's criticizing, understand, is COLORED speech, Allison's mother probably dialing in to complain on a regular basis. "Now listen here, Principal Fisk. My Allison never brought home worse than B plus under Miss Ticson. Now it's C minus, C minus, C minus. How do you explain that? I'll tell you how I explain it. That new substitute you hired. Kids can't understand a word she's saying. How can kids learn if they can't understand a thing the teacher's saying?"

The principal's reply? "Truth is, Mrs. Avery's the better teacher." Or: "Had to hire one of them, Mrs. Ferrell. State required it."

Toss up, man, toss up.

But before Mrs. Avery can respond to here and now impertinence, before Jocelyn can do us all a favor and snap Allison's neck, there's a knock on the door. Too faint a tap to be Principal Fisk himself—principals who bother to knock never knock timid. A surprise visitor, all the same.

Wayne in his oily overalls.

Nell looks at me, I look at her, both of us knowing it can't be anything but bad, bad news for Lucian, who's closed his eyes again, enjoying a little midmorning catnap. And me thinking, just this side of hoping, that whatever Clarence has done, maybe it's done him in. That maybe this time is the last time Lucian will get called out of a classroom, called home, called in to clean up, fix and finish what Clarence started, square things with the law, smooth the ruffled, soothe the rattled.

"Lucian?"

So Lucian opens his eyes, and before Nell can reach over to touch his arm he's up and moving, clued by the messenger, Wayne waiting patient but sheepish, hands shoved hard into those overall pockets, dreading, got to be, what he's come to share.

"It's that crazy daddy of his, count on it," Allison mocks and Nell whirls round, quick as a striking copperhead.

"One more fucking word and I swear to God that tongue of yours bleeds."

Which ought to make Jocelyn at least harrump support, but no, Jocelyn's still rage-rigid, eyes glittery, fuming about that earlier mouth-off.

Too little too late, Nell's blow-up, far as Jocelyn's concerned.

The second Allison starting talking trash to Mrs. Avery, showing disrespect—that's when Nell should have threatened tongue damage.

But she didn't.

Because she's a white girl.

Just like Allison.

She didn't, Jocelyn would say, because white'll fight for white but never on behalf of COLORED.

Clarence

In the dark on this one too. Had no idea Wayne had run off to fetch Lucian. Thought he'd gone on back inside the garage, back to work, after poking his head out, glancing up at me straddling that pitch of post office roof. I waved, he waved, otherwise too busy patching flats or greasing dry axles to bother with Clarence Carter shenanigans, I figured. And he should have kept busy minding garage business stead of hightailing it to the high school.

Harrison's little sneak-in wish? My exit hurried along for Lucian's sake? I heard the sentiment. Perked these dead ears right up. Hurtful but a done deal, so let's move on.

What I'd learned from previous high jinks, I put to use in that post office caper. One, if a person ain't around to see the effect of his put-on, he gives away all the fun. Two, if he ain't there to gauge reaction, how's he gonna see how to go one better next time? Understand what I'm getting at? Rooftop performance made perfect sense because they see me, I see them seeing me, both sides get a ringside seat. Just perching atop a post office, though, that wouldn't by itself cause folks to stand around gawking, mouths open to flies. So I took my gun up with me to pick off some starlings.

Damn too many of those pests in Mawatuck. Ask anybody.

Crazy man on a roof taking potshots at starlings captures the public's imagination. Sure it does.

Oh, Lawd, Iris. You see him up there? Waving that gun?

What's he gonna do?

Shoot himself? Shoot us?

Just to be clear: anyone crazy or sane opens fire on his own kind, himself included, that's the end of his mischief-making. And while I'm in the business of contradicting rumors, I'll say this too: when Miz Rainey opened the door to me in my birthday suit, she did scream, yes she did. Screamed and *threatened* to faint, but, point of fact stayed upright, peeking, entire time, through the lace of her fancy handkerchief. That detail about falling to the rug, that got added in later by somebody after a better yarn.

Soon as I climb up on the P.O. roof, Jonas Kassing drives up in his pickup, so intent on checking a shredded windshield wiper I have to hound-whistle before he'll look up.

But he responds to whistle. Nothing wrong with Jonas's hearing. It's his knees that're shot.

"Clarence, you blame fool, whachu doing up there?"

"Smelling the breeze," say I.

"No breeze this time of year, Clarence."

"Not only do I feel a breeze, Jonas, I feel a *glory* breeze, cool and *contagious*."

That's all it takes to lose Jonas.

"Crazy coot."

And off he goes.

Next arrivals: cousins Sadie and Minnie Powell. Generous-sized women in dresses with hardworking seams. Minnie's the one spies me first.

"Greetings, ladies."

Gasp like they've been hornet stung, but stay riveted to the spot.

Fun loses some of its luster when Sis roars up in her Buick, dressed in town clothes, that I'll admit.

Don't like being taken unawares, Sis don't. Not a bit.

"Your brother's been up there for...how long you 'spect, Sadie? Half hour? Three-quarters?"

"Clarence Augustus!"

"Sister of mine. Aren't you looking fine this fine, fine day."

Splotchy is what she looks, splotchy on the way to radish red. You know the color I'm referencing. So red it's almost purple. But no sense announcing that to Sis or the world.

Dolled up, she can't easily shimmy up beside me for a private chitchat. Which leaves her the last place on earth she wants to be: hip to hip with Powell riffraff while she bluster-pleads with her shameless brother.

"Clarence Augustus, you ignoring the request of your only sister? Your closest blood kin?"

Awfully attached to that blood kin line. Throws it in every chance she gets, you notice. Spinsters are a clingy brood. It's a fact to accept, not fight.

"Hold out your pocketbook, Sis. Let's see if I can pick it off."

Doing her a favor, I figure. Witness to my starling success, the Powell cousins hear that invite, scatter wide as buckshot itself.

Is Irene grateful? Pins that tiny clutch bag to her chest and squalls: "You shoot anything of mine it'll be this aggrieved heart. Go ahead, brother. Finish the job you've started."

Saw it then, see it now: how pleased Sis is by that speech, the sound of her own voice. Not a half-beat later, she's got that martyred sister role down pat, on her knees in post office gravel, sacrificing nylons, encouraging all grades of riffraff to pat at her burdened shoulders. Working together like a team rehearsed, Sis and me, when suddenly I hear the wind-down of a too familiar engine. On the road, turning in, a turquoise Fairlaine with my boy behind the wheel, Wayne following close in his wrecker, both vehicles coming to a standstill in the P.O. driveway.

Didn't want Lucian showing up at the post office, didn't want him at Miz Rainey's either, searching her tulip patch for my underwear. Not his job to get me back in my drawers or off a rooftop, either.

Irene leaps up, nylons shredded, rushing in Lucian's direction, but he's got no time or temper for his Aunt Irene.

To me, he calls up: "Hey, Daddy."

Even before I was dead, I felt that greeting like a screwdriver to the ribs. The blunt hurt of it. The hard fate of my boy trying to do right by me and his absent mother, called out of his classroom graduation week, called upon to show the sense his daddy lacks.

"Lucian, son, no need for you to be here. Your daddy's got it covered."

"A little too covered, looks like. Wanna unload that rife?"

Even so inclined I couldn't have finished that dumping before Donnie Anderson's squad car nosed past Wayne's wrecker. Delighted by that law presence myself because a badge and uniform on the scene always guarantees there'll be a report filed, a report for snooping taxmen to read.

"If you clear the parking lot, I'll get him down."

"Sorry, Lucian. Your daddy's picked the wrong building for target practice. Federal property is federal property."

"He's not going to shoot anybody."

"You believe that, I believe that, but the sheriff might have a different take. Then it's my ass in a vise."

Irene circling that twosome like a mole blocked from its main tunnel.

"I'll thank you to watch your language, deputy. Lady present."

"Beg pardon," Donnie says.

"Go home, Irene," is what Lucian says. "We'll see to Daddy."

"And not be here when Clarence decides to jump!?!"

"I ain't gonna jump, Sis."

Can't allow folks to build up hopes *that* high, then disappoint.

"You want me to go around back with a ladder?" Wayne ventures.

"He climbed up using a magnolia tree, he can climb down using a magnolia tree," Lucian snaps, frustrated by all and sundry. "Long as anybody's watching, Daddy won't budge. Ya'll know that, don't you?"

"Lucian Carter!"

"What NOW, Irene?"

"Your daddy's got his troubles, but to hear his own flesh and blood say he's doing this all for SHOW!!!"

And here's where Donnie proves how he earns his keep. Steps in, steps between, works his deputy con on Irene, convincing Sis he's gotta have her help, can't clear that parking lot without her.

"People respect what you say, Irene. They'll listen to you quicker than they will me."

Fluffed and flattered, Sis suddenly can't do enough to aid and abet Deputy Don, shoving and shooing off my audience like it's a homework assignment.

But until Eliza Morgan returns to sorting mail, Wayne to squirting grease, Sis to her Buick under deputy escort, Lucian stays put. Only after that clear-out does he climb up far enough to take the gun and leave me with two hands free to follow.

When I let go that last limb, magnolia petals and fragrance drop with me.

Embarrassment is partly why I blurt what I do. Merrying up that seriousness is the other. Tapping the magnolia trunk between us, I tease: "That oak in our yard proves useless, I can always use this one for a neck swing."

Boy of mine doesn't smile, doesn't frown, doesn't blink—doesn't anymore give so much as a hot damn what his daddy does or doesn't do with his neck—that's the hard sum of it.

Worn out from caring, him and his mama. Just slam worn out.

Harrison

Nell says: "You mind giving me a ride home? Lucian was supposed to. But."

Big *but*, that one. Neither of us wise to its precise cause.

Dreading enlightenment, actually.

After final bell, Jocelyn sees the two of us walking towards the Firebird. Jimmy Barnard and that bunch see us too. If looks could kill, dead and buried this boy would be. Nell, she pays no attention. Walking head down, hair in her eyes, nibbling fingernail, everything in that brain and body devoted to Lucian worry.

In the car, she says: "So what's your prediction? What's Clarence done now?"

No way I'm speculating on that score.

"Must be pretty awful, though." Most of that mumble directed at window glass. Talking to be talking. Talking like she hopes talk will help in the figure out.

Which it won't.

Which she herself knows, deep down.

"I mean, for Wayne to leave the garage and all."

"Uh-huh."

What else is there to say? Minor awful, major awful, we've both got to wait to find out where Clarence's latest registers on the awful scale.

Almost at the Bull Run turnoff when she reaches over, starts picking at my sleeve.

"Stop a minute."

Steer the Firebird toward shoulder grass, hoping to hell nobody white, especially white in a pickup, drives by and spots Nell Stallings in my passenger seat.

"Will you check with Wayne? Let me know what he says?"

"Heading that way now."

"Good."

Nothing good about Nell Stallings loitering in my car.

Nothing.

"I could get out here, walk the rest of the way. Save you the detour."

"Sounds like a plan."

Encouraging, prompting, but those scoot-along hints—not getting picked up on.

Un-a.

"Okay then—see you."

"Yeah. Okay."

Hand still planted on the door handle, rest of her stalled too, frowning, brooding and me checking, checking, checking the rearview mirror because empty road won't, can't, stay empty long. Somebody's going to drive by, see us, tell the world we were screwing, black on white, black in white, broad daylight. That's the tale they always tell on teenagers, true or not.

"And afterwards you'll stop by Lucian's? See how he's doing?"

"After a while...maybe."

"Right. Yeah. Lucian's probably not wild for company just yet."

Not wild, positively opposed, I'd guess, but how can you discuss daddy fuck-ups with a daddy-less girl?

"So...then...we're set," I say.

"But you'll definitely let me know?"

"Soon as I have something to tell."

That gets her out.

Don't even wait for her to start walking, man. Me and that Firebird tearing off from cockleburs, wheels spinning, fighting for traction, finding it on asphalt, speeding off like there's a lynch mob on our ass.

On our ass and gaining, man, gaining.

Clarence

Solemn ride in that Ford, long one too, measured not in miles but silence from the P.O. to Carter alley, Lucian navigating home turf ruts with a minimal of chassis slam. No temple cleaner than that Fairlaine's dashboard and instruments, outside grill nearly as. Lucian missing from the house, nine times out of ten you'd find him squatting, sponge in hand, bathing and buffing whitewalls.

Never inquired how he got and paid for that automobile and he didn't confide. Knew the boy hadn't STOLE the car—showed it off too much for that. Now that I'm in on how Wayne salvaged what some owner dumped on the canal road, I feel a little kinder toward the mechanic.

A little kinder, not a bunch.

Expert driving, low gear, none of that fends off dust. Swirling up and over the hood, floating down on chrome and windshield glass. First clue I'm in for a discussion I've got no use for: Lucian ignoring that swirl.

Sure enough, Ford glides to a stop not a fart's scent from where that government Plymouth burned oil.

"Before you get out..."

"Make it quick, son. Your daddy's been on that rooftop awhile."

Reach over to ruffle his head hair but a hand shoots up to thwart that funning.

"This has to stop."

"Too old for hair ruffling, are you?"

Not that a body could tell. Hanging down over his ears, untended as Carter fields.

"I'm not talking HAIR."

"Then you best speak plainer. I ain't familiar with a 'this.' "

Stomach growling, bladder full as a nursing teat.

"This game. This constant notice-me crap."

Didn't like his tone. Didn't like his tone a-tall. A son ought not to use that tone, I don't care what his daddy's done or not done. Carrying on like he's the one laying down the law stead of vice versa.

"Who you quotin' now? Irene?"

"Occasionally even Irene calls it right."

Taut bladder'll make you an ornery cuss. Add provocation to the mix, man loses all inclination to pacify.

"What you suggesting, boy? Your daddy ought to buckle under? Attempt to pay what he don't have? What he don't OWE?"

"Everybody has to pay taxes. Clarence Carter included."

"Even piss poor people?" Bladder problem proclaiming itself every which-a-way. "I don't think so. I don't think so."

"Then quit for Mama's sake."

"Don't be talking to me about your mama's sake. She understands what I'm doing and why. Agrees with me too."

"Horse shit."

"Watch your mouth."

"Don't have fucking time, Daddy. Too busy watching out for your fucking ass."

That slap up side the head makes his neck, then his knuckles, blush. No regrets. You can't let a young'un mouth off to his daddy and get clean away with it.

"Next thing, you'll be claiming I'm upsetting Irene."

"Screw Irene."

"You angling for another slap?"

Because a slur on family women, aggravating as those women might be—that's worse than daddy sass.

"Belt you another, I will."

Huffing and puffing I was and clueless that Lucian came close as he'd ever come to hitting back hard and fast. And if he had, I guarantee, benefit of hindsight, his daddy would have lost that round. Big men get used to thinking the biggest stay the biggest till somebody comes along and makes it bruising clear otherwise.

"You're not listening. You never listen."

"Listen to what? You give directions?"

"It's too much, Daddy. Can't you see that? Besides worrying about where you are and what you're up to, Mama's got to sit through Irene's version of what if. Live with Mawatuck morons feeling sorry for *her*."

Offended on his mama's behalf, see, but all I could think is *uh-huh, Rosie does have some of that Lily high-horse in her.*

"People shove you in this life, son, occasionally you gotta shove back. Else you're lost as a cow in a snowstorm."

"You're making things worse."

"I ain't making things worse!"

"You are. And the hurt's spreading."

Won't name himself victim of that spreading hurt 'cause some of what floods his veins is prideful Arnold blood too. A classroom full of seniors watched his back this morning. Tomorrow morning that same crew's going to peer at his face, wondering, speculating. That's what he's dreading: showing up, staring down those stares as crazy Clarence's pitiable son.

You fail people the livelong day. That's what being dead teaches too late to mend your ways. Not one big failure all at once. More like pieces of gravel rolling up against each other in a riverbed, single mistakes joining together until they dam up whatever trust and good will and affection once flowed freely in your direction.

A misery-causing man, I was and am, dead and reliving.

Mabel

"I said keep still, Missy! Else you'll get a knee full of straight pins!"

Demand she stand on the kitchen table so I won't have to stoop to catch up her frock hem, but what help's that when the girl's almost twice blinded me, twitching a bony knee?

"I've been standing up here for hours!"

Exaggerates worse than a mockingbird.

"Just leave the thing loopy. The robe'll cover it. Who cares if the hem's straight, anyway? Not me."

"I'm not sending you out in public with a scalloped hem! Not as long as I've got fingers and a needle. "

Throws up her arms, throwing off the pleat line *again*.

"Go ahead. Make it more a trial than it is."

"Can we at least take a BREAK?"

"And give you chance to spill something on yourself? Turn this white into running stains?"

"I know. A white dress. Real practical, huh? I bet Mrs. Broome made up the so-called tradition. To torture girls."

"Boys aren't wearing white?"

"White shirts, but not white PANTS. Not white SHOES. How am I supposed to get here to there and stay *white*?"

Something to that qualm. Unless she travels plastic-wrapped.

"Fucking graduation."

"Clean up that mouth, Missy, or you'll be feeling a pin prick somewhere besides kneecap."

"Sorry. But it's true—about graduation. Being overblown."

"People don't get handed diplomas everyday."

"Yeah, yeah. A real special occasion."

"Rate we're progressing, I'll be following you across that special stage, still sewing."

What the young will take serious as salt—never any telling. One second to the next, fidgets vanish. Feel her eyes boring into this grey head from above.

"Are you serious?"

"About getting this hem straight?"

"About following me onstage."

"If I have to."

"Would you, really? Come to baccalaureate, I mean?"

"Traipse all the way to Mawatuck gym to sit on a hard bleacher and listen to a preacher?"

"The preacher's not the main attraction, I am. And you'd get to see me in my dopey tassel cap."

"Seeing plenty of you right now, Missy. And a lot more comfortable than I would in a hot gym."

"Maaaa-bel..."

"Don't Ma-bel me. These bones are too old for such hardship."

Yanks the hem out of my hands, needle still in it, jumps to the floor, strips down to her slip tail, eyes flashing like pinwheels.

"Every time you don't want to do something you use that excuse."

"No excuse, young'un. Fact. One you don't like hearing, but a fact regardless."

"Here's another. You've got one granddaughter. ONE. And she's got one graduation. ONE."

Much as I don't like admitting it, the girl's got good reason to bridle. Talking out of both sides of my mouth is what I've been doing. Pushing graduation's importance but putting no effort in proving it. Leaving Rose Carter to represent the Stallings family as well as the Carters, the only kin in that audience for Amelia Nell to give a wave to.

"Where're you going?"

Last time I went rummaging through this packed closet Zion Baptist hadn't hired the dullest preacher ever graced a pulpit. Lord's not a fan of dullness. Doesn't expect His creatures to be.

"Mabel!"

"I'll find something in here I can still get round my waist."

Damp fingers pulling at my arm ain't helping that search a bit.

"Mabel, stop. Don't."

"Might need a little altering, but I'll make it fit. I still got time."

"Will you just STOP? PLEASE? Those bleachers *are* torture. You'd come home with a backache for sure."

"I can survive a backache, Amelia Nell."

If she hadn't been pestering and clutching at me, getting in my way, blocking the light, I would have recognized what was on that hanger before snatching it out and flapping it in air between us.

Young'un never should have seen that garment, formal as the burial it was bought for, not even a glimpse.

"Quit fighting me, Amelia Nell!"

"YOU quit! What I said, when I said it, I was just thinking about me. Me wanting you there to see me...I don't know, trip on a plastic runner."

"You won't trip. And whether you do or don't, your grandmamma ought to bear witness."

"I don't NEED a witness. I was just being selfish, okay? No one who doesn't HAVE to be there, should be. It's going to be endless. I KNOW. I've PRACTICED."

Shove that funeral wear as far back as it will shove into a closet that now seems too much like a ground hole that should have stayed dark and undisturbed till the Lord's Second Coming. Material between my fingers no more than an instant, but long enough to release again its scent of grief.

"I'm sorry. I'm so sorry."

Skinny arms winding round, hugging tight.

"I've upset you for nothing."

Drags me the three feet between hallway and my bed, bedcovers strewn with magazines, seed catalogs, wire cutters. Makes me sit facing a row of potted begonias that can't for all their spread entirely block out the old woman in the mirror, hair the color of hanging moss, skin wrinkled as washboard.

"This is one of those times you need a mama, Amelia Nell. To clap alongside all the other mamas."

"Mabel, *please*! I don't need a mama. What I need is a mouth bolt. I'm a total crabapple today. I don't know why."

But now that I stop attending so much to Mabel Stallings, start attending a little more to the Stallings in my care, seems to me she's got a pretty fair notion.

"You fretting about tripping on plastic, falling flat on your face?"

"No. Well. A little."

"Some other school trouble?"

Sigh that windy, you know you've hit close.

"I guess you could say it *started* at school."

"You going to have to do better than that, Missy."

"Okay, but if I tell you, don't start yelling at me. Okay? Because I didn't keep it from you. Not on purpose. Not exactly."

"This your way of testing curiosity or patience?"

Another sigh. Gale force.

"Okay. Yesterday? Wayne had to come get Lucian out of class—because of Clarence."

"Clarence doing what?"

"Climbing on top of the post office. With a gun."

"Who told you this? Wayne?"

"Harrison, actually. But Wayne told him. Since the garage is practically next door to the post office, I guess Wayne saw everything from the beginning. Or close to it, anyway."

Not all that young himself, Cousin Clarence. Slip, fall, break his neck. Forget the taxmen. Where would that leave Rose and Lucian?

"Clarence better keep his performing ground level."

"Yeah, well, he didn't."

"Naked again?"

That got a lemon-sucking lip twist.

"I don't *think* so."

"Then don't keep me in suspense, young'un. Did or didn't Lucian get him down before the shooting started?"

"Clarence might have fired on a few starlings before Lucian and Donnie got there. But Lucian's Aunt Irene beat them both. According to Wayne."

God help the lot of them, Irene Carter in the mix, squealing the whole time like she'd been moccasin-bit. Lay money it was Rainey Moss called up the sheriff's office, payback for Clarence's last escapade.

A mess. Been a mess. Rose living in a jumble town of Carter shacks, peeing in a slop jar, wondering what her husband'll do next. "A woman in love doesn't care about plumbing, Cousin Mabel"—new bride talk, new bride full of blush and hope that her mama will soften to a son-in-law's charms. "You wait and see, Cousin Mabel. Mama'll come around."

Still waiting for that miracle, Rose must be. Lily thought the Carters were trash long before Clarence mixed crazy in the stream.

"If you could have seen his face, Mabel. Lucian's, I mean. When he got up from that desk. Like he was preparing himself for anything."

Tandem sighing now.

Because it's not right: a young'un shouldering that kind of responsibility. Trying to keep between his daddy and the law, his daddy and government snoops. Clarence too wrapped up in his own bamboozling to notice his son's frantic fancy stepping.

"You talked to Lucian today?"

"Not about YESTERDAY. I wouldn't dare. I just sort of insisted we go to The Lido tonight. Even though it's Tuesday. To get him, you know, out of the house.... Is that okay? Me going out tonight?"

"Little late to be asking now, Missy."

Because this very second those Fairlaine tires are churning up my driveway's oyster shells, dusting my hydrangea hedge.

"Oh shit. We can finish tomorrow, can't we, Mabel? Can't we?"

Anxious, anxious.

The pair of them. Born to or bred in worry, not half as protected as the Lord intended.

Harrison

That idea of Nell's? Lido on a Tuesday night?

When she marches herself and that suggestion round to the smoking wall, insisting Jimmy Barnard and the rest join the caravan, nobody says, even as a mock: "You coming too, Harrison? Come on. What's say we do some Lido integrating about nine tonight?"

No ha-ha's flung in any direction, Tuesday a.m. Not a soul even *considering* quizzing Lucian on daddy.

What happened, jack? What got your papa off that roof? Donnie Anderson's badge or your Aunt Irene's fake swoon? Did the deputy and your old man shoot it out? Did the law bleed?

Well shit then.

Shit.

Hardly worth the gawk, sounds like.

Yesterday afternoon, soon as I'm home, Mama started asking what ailed me—ME.

"Do we need to talk, Harrison?"

Talk's Mama's specialty. Diehard believer in discussion and why I'd love to know. What's talk ever done for her, got her?

She and Daddy, hostess and host, kitchen chairs wedged between living room furniture to seat all that eager blackness dressed in their "something momentous" clothes—suits, ties, ladies in nylons. Sipped coffee, downed pound cake with peach sauce, Mama handing out seconds to the fat and nearly so. "Certainly there's more. Plenty to go round again."

More *food*, more *dessert*, but not too much other plenty to be found in Mawatuck County if you were at Jean and Furillo's house meeting.

What we need is to run someone for office. Commissioner, sheriff.

What we need is to sign up the black vote.
Sign it up, then get it out.
Make a difference.
Have some IMPACT.

Hiding in the hallway, in my pjs, spying on that excitement feed. Each one jazzing the next, glorying in the shine-on of opportunity, what they could do, what it would mean, jiggle dancing in their seats, everybody agreeing harder, louder, faster till someone stopped to take a breath—that's all it took, just that littlest space of silence, that fraction of quiet, for obstacles real and imagined to wet blanket that circle, come down sop-heavy on those dreamers and their dreams.

Wait a minute, wait a minute. Even if we got every black voter registered and at the polls, even if every one of us voted as a bloc, that's not enough, is it?

To defeat a white sheriff? To darken up that pasty Board of Commissioners?

Huh.

Sentences left dangling, demands for justice petering out faster than Mawatuck snowflakes. And then Mama collecting dishes, Daddy gathering coats, both of them exchanging keep-the-faith/we-shall-overcome goodbyes at the door. The two of them alone, murmuring at the sink, last cup and saucer dried and back in the cupboard. Again and again and again, that's what they did, all they did: start with talk, end with talk, get nowhere in between.

Jocelyn McPherson would have a theory about that.

If I asked.

Which I don't.

That generation? Too old and tired and set in their ways. Afraid of drastic, afraid to try, because they're old and tired and set in their ways.

Uh-huh.

Reason in the round.

How's that different from talk that ends as talk?

And what's Jocelyn herself done that's so fucking drastic? Transfer with the rest of us from Central. Frown, fume and flare that horse nose. Belittle idiots like Allison Ferrell and Melinda Larson.

How's that add up to bad-ass brave?

"Harrison? Was there some kind of...incident? At school?"

Questioning that careful meant Mama assumed it was a black and white "incident," a white versus black thing. Also meant gossip about Clarence and his gun on the post office roof had spread slower than usual.

Only part I blabbed was Lucian getting yanked from school, and to that Mama said: "Shame in this world."

Because Mama likes Lucian well enough, other two in that household less.

Around twilight, I said: "Enough time has passed. I figure it's okay to venture over."

"You think that's wise?"

Expression hid behind the refrigerator's door, a crusty package from the freezer on its way to heat up and supper, but I knew by her tone what she was thinking.

THINKING, but would never/no-how say aloud.

Don't you go over there! There's a big white crazy man on the loose at that house! No telling what he'll do! To his family! To you! You stay put, sugar. Here. In this house. Where it's safe.

And what's so safe about our house, I'd like to know?

Brick solid?

So?

White men have burnt down houses of brick as well as houses of wood. Mama herself has seen it happen. More than once.

"I won't stay long."

Other side of the ditch, Carter side, was eerie quiet. Nobody answered my ultra-polite call either.

"Lucian? Hey, Lucian? You around? Miz Carter? Mr. Clarence?"

Nothing, man. Not even a chicken squawk.

Circled the house twice, chicken coop too, listened hard for a Clarence giggle coming from somewhere close but it wasn't around, man. Near or far. Just wasn't there. Tractor was there, parked sideways, next to the clothesline. But not the Fairlaine: front of the house, back of the house, back of the barn, not a speck of turquoise.

Made me think I'd heard Wayne wrong the first time. Maybe Donnie didn't leave Clarence for Lucian's handling. Maybe the deputy had charged Clarence with disturbing the peace, stashed him in a cell barely big enough for a squirt like Mitchell Sears, forced Clarence to cool his heels while Donnie talked charges and fines with Lucian and his mama.

"Naw," Wayne said to all that. "Naw. Clarence went home with Lucian."

Bring up that stuff? With Lucian? Tuesday early or late?

Un-a.

Pretended with the rest of them in that smoking line everything was same ole, same ole. That Lido suggestion of Nell's? Ordinary as earthworms. Tuesday night at The Lido? Nothing strange, nothing peculiar, nothing off about *that*.

Un-a.

But soon as I get in the Firebird, start driving, even the sky looks off. Darker than it should be, this hour. Too many gulls hovering thick, in flocks, above Mawatuck Bridge. Ocean too calm even for night. And me perched on a dune, watching how sand just lays there. Takes whatever ocean dishes out. Rolled on and over a million times a million.

Dozen years ago, black folk didn't lounge on this particular strip of beat-on sand, daytime or nighttime. Drove all the way to Coquina to stretch out a towel or bed sheet. Packed our own fried chicken, deviled eggs, Pepsi colas and cupcakes. Packed a picnic, man, or went hungry. No restaurant along the way willing to serve *us* sit-down.

Our beach Coquina—supposed to be.

Except a bunch of us looked up one day from sand-castle-ing and here comes beachcombers with skin nowhere near the color of charcoal.

Virginians, probably, judging by how long it took them to notice us peppering up the shoreline, the dogs with them faster on the uptake, snapping, growling, raring to rip into our skinny black calves.

Dogs think they're the color of whoever owns them.

It's a fact.

Even on a black beach, whites have the right-a-way, whites and their any color dogs.

Band's playing sluggish tonight. Probably always the case, Tuesdays. Too few customers to rev up for.

Jimmy. Pick him out full moon or none. Slouch mixed with dart, hands full of something besides his own meat bone. Setting up early for break time, don't you bet, getting ready on those backstairs with some rolled or loose inspiration. Help the brothers get through this boring gig.

Special "musician's" price.

Huh.

So where's skinhead Leroy? Off skulking about? Off somewhere maiming somebody? Not guarding the entrance. Not circling the parking lot. Maybe Tuesday's vacation night for Leroy. Maybe Boss figures: so what if twenty kids riot? How much damage can twenty drunk kids do? *Somebody* must be guzzling up there, second floor. Got to be.

Here to those entrance doors?

Beach bucket throw, no farther.

Bowling pin man could sprint that distance in no time flat—him or his ghost.

Should have bought a bag off Jimmy myself this afternoon. Used it to mellow out, forget yellow lights, relax out of this hunker down, avoid a charley horse.

"Don't strain! You'll give yourself a charley horse!" Mama used to call to Daddy, pushing the lawnmower. And in my head, they got mixed: charley horse, seahorse. Seahorse named Charley. Every trip to

Coquina, searched for a seahorse souvenir and gold doubloons, lost pirate booty.

Local celebrity now, Blackbeard, but you think Edward Teach and his snaky beard got invited to tea and cookies back when? Found a porch full of welcome baskets every time he dry-docked?

History, man, it's a nip and tuck game. That thing you think happened? Half happened, happened different, never happened at all. Take that first day we got bussed in, dropped off by the cafeteria. When that story's told, down the road, somebody's going to claim there was blood spilt, some white, more black.

You wait.

Tale minus blood and blows, nobody listens, remembers.

Can't trust the past. Can't....SHIT!

Where the fuck they come from? Out of nowhere, man.

Nell mumbling: *You did!* and *What else could you...*

Both of them plopping down closer than mid-court to foul line.

Shit.

"On another topic entirely—how'd Mabel take to the waitress idea?"

"Like strychnine."

"'Listen here, young'un. There's more to the world than Mawatuck County. Now get out there and have yourself a gander.' Did I nail it word for word?"

"Pretty much."

"Miss Amelia Nell Stallings, off to see the world. Never left a chair she wasn't kicked out of, but off to see the world."

"Oh yeah? Oh YEAH? Watch THIS!"

And Nell's up and running, back and forth and back and forth, until she freeze-stops, screams.

Fucking moonlight, man. Fucking flashbulb moon.

Lucian shoots off sand like he's been cannon fired, scanning for danger unidentified.

"Chill, you two. It's me."

"Shit, Harrison!"/"Harrison, Jesus!"/"Where'd you come from, man?"

Both yakking at once.

"Public beach, ain't it?"

"Of course...just didn't expect..."

"Expected or not, here I am."

"See that, NOW. But you might have called out. Let us know you were here," Lucian says, less afraid of hurting my black boy feelings since I've done the unforgivable: scared Nell.

"It's not Harrison's fault, it's mine. I don't know why I screamed."

But she does know, just like I know and Lucian knows too. But who of the three's going to admit it?

Stand here all our lives waiting for that confession to pop.

The roach we share? Like passing a peace pipe without the Indians.

"Band's startin' up."

"Let it," Nell says, both of them ignoring that callback.

"Music sounds just as good from here," Lucian says without losing too much inhale.

"Plus no Allison, no Melinda, no fucking Jimmy Barnard," Nell says.

"Suit yourself. I'm elsewhere, man."

Off in Firebird direction, except I don't get there.

What's it take them? One minute? Three? Before they get up, stroll back toward their all-white Lido?

Dope, man. Sets up a feedback echo. Every thought twice around, slower, amplified.

So.

So...WHAT?

Black boy slinking off, driving home, tail tucked.

Un-a.

Not going to happen, man.

Not AGAIN.

Not TONIGHT.

Going IN this time. Though that screen door, up those stairs, out onto that dance floor.

On the move.

Bound for Lido Land.

You watch.

You watch, man.

Just you stand back and fucking watch me.

Clarence

Some things need to be said here, quick things.

Harrison was barreling headfirst for trouble, you see that. Boss and his buds weren't about to let anyone, black or white, defy the rules of their roadhouse and skirt hurt in the bargain. Wasn't a likelihood, wasn't even a possibility.

The dead are sore tempted to interfere, do what we're not supposed to: prevent the about-to from happening to save people we love from harm. If I'd been dead then, overseeing Harrison use that sand dune for starting line, about to plunge himself and my boy and Cousin Mabel's grandyoung'un into a whirlpool of injury, maybe I'd have caused him to pause on that threshold or, failing that, lent him a pair of black flying wings, Leroy bearing down hard.

But even confessing the urge to meddle, I know what happened had to. Harrison had to show himself he could storm The Lido, prove the same to that nagging black girl, the one full of instruction on what should rile him on his people's behalf. Had to because of a kid in pajamas, hiding in nighttime hallways, listening to elders stuck in firebrand talk. Had to because his color wasn't automatically invited to Mawatuck High School, because first time on that schoolyard favoring the green- and blue-eyed, his welcome had been less than warm and four years later, truth be told, it'd scarcely heated.

Slower than an overturned jar of honey, the world's progress. A pace grievous to abide if you got a bit of young blood in you, if you're a boy youth-strong and feeling that strength in your loins and chest, body and brain both urging fight and conquer.

Knuckle-headed as Harrison's party crash might have been, I got a lot of respect for his actions, Tuesday, close to midnight. He'd never countenance the compare but, same as Clarence Carter, he took on a boss, reminded people rules that make no sense are rules destined for resistance. Just takes one somebody, refusing to sit back, salute and obey, just one to start a change.

Harrison

Up close those screen doors are full of holes big enough for elephant mosquitoes to zoom through. What's not a hole, bulged from nudging.

No nudging from these elbows.

Flat out shoving.

Shoving through.

Soda fountain to the left, empty except for a wise-ass potato chip owl, winking.

Think I wink back? At fucking cardboard?

Fry's the odor: burgers, potatoes, meat grease. Pool chalk can't overcome fry, even if someone was chalking a cue.

Breathing hard for nothing.

Swallowing nervous for nothing.

Eight ball eyeing me—that's it. Left, right, backwards, forwards, pivot once, pivot again, scanning. Peering hard in every corner, trying to find someone peering back, take notice of who the hell just barrel-assed in.

Shit.

Ceiling muffles the music. Ruins the beat line. Band sounds fine from a sand dune, but in here...

Shit.

Relying on that beat to get me up stairs, two at a time, three. A little assist from the brothers on stage.

Only way to do it is do it rush. Act like those stairs are center court to backboard. Run, jump, scramble, turn sharp, straight on toward check-in fluorescence. Straight up to Boss's cash-counting, wattle-necked cashier.

Finally.

A pair of beady eyes to take in this black boy on the charge.

There goes the cashbox. Dropped out of sight/out of reach because a black man running fast and hard is always a black man out to rob, right?

Buzzer.

Shit.

Pretty fast hands for an ancient white woman.

But mine are faster. Snatch that purple stamp. Apply.

Shit.

Purple on black.

Shit.

Hardly shows.

So where's fast Leroy? Him and rest of Boss's bouncer clan? Those bastards actually *waiting* till I get a sway going to a bored band's song?

Except that bored band? Not so bored all of a sudden. Kicking up the volume. Playing loud enough to cover bouncer whacks.

Hey. HEY BROTHERS!

Looking elsewhere, man. Not even slightly tempted to lose their fee for a black and purple gatecrasher in Boss's kingdom by the sea.

On your OWN, brother.

And how.

Because here he comes. Like a mad ape let loose from his backroom cage, pounding down the side row, planning to scoop me up like a piece of black grit, like a pickaninny shirking fieldwork unless I now, now, NOW window dive, sacrifice a leg to save neck.

But, shit, man, shit, not just Leroy.

Lucian, Nell, running too because they see me, see Leroy, see the gap closing, see me standing still as a fool, giving every advantage to a man needs none.

Just like he was pitching for wall, man.

Exactly like.

Lobbing black and purple, waiting to hear it splat.

"Amelia Nell!"

But she's already clawing toward the top of Leroy's head, gouging at his eyes with those gnawed off fingernails.

Too many in too many directions for Lucian to save: Nell, me, himself.

"Harrison, watch out!"

"NOOOOOOOO!"

But it's done, man, it's done, I'm flying, flying with no wall behind me, flying in for a crash land.

"Get that nigger out of here. Get the jigaboo out."

Boss. Must be. Making a rare appearance. The Bossman himself come out to damn my hide. Where's the fucking camera when you need one, man? Proof to flash in Jocelyn McPherson's face.

Yeah.

Yeah.

Split lip smiling, bones rattled but in one piece.

Yeah.

Can't wait, can't wait to say: "Hey, GIRL! You got any idea what you missed, Tuesday night, Lido? Harrison Doxey delivering a wake-up call to the Bossman himself. Top of the stairs, second floor. Uh-huh. This black boy got all the way up. Sure did. Had himself a look around. Gave the Bossman his first bad dream."

Because where one jigaboo goes, more will follow.

Right, Jocelyn? Right?

Harrison Doxey, fucking pioneer.

So there.

Bitch.

There.

Remind me again *your* fucking claim to fame?

Clarence

I'm just witness. Seeing what the dead see. Hearing what the dead hear. Grieving what the dead grieve over: how the done and finished still feels fresh and surprising, full of pain and turmoil, to those in the muck and mire of it.

I'm with Lucian now if not then, riding shotgun as the Fairlaine turns up Carter lane in the dark of morning, Methuselah with 969 years' worth of disappointments no more burdened than my boy this hour. Eases out of the driver's seat, shirt sleeve torn, nasty bump on the noggin, lights a cigarette, turns to peer at stars like those bright beams might hold some of the answers he's searching for and can't discover. But stars fail him. Sky and moon and stars all fail him.

For longer than I'd believe, you telling this to me, he sits on the front steps, smoking. Just Lucian, quiet and still, running through his worry list: Harrison, his mama, me, Amelia Nell, 60 acres of barren soil, that Lido dust up, over and over again, blaming himself for studying a beer can, for listening to Amelia Nell chatter, for the chair switch that let him escape Melinda's doe eyes but put his back to the stairs, for not reacting sooner to the buzzer that set all the rest in motion—the band's switch from plunk to full out pound, Leroy darting from a backroom, running full tilt toward a blackness that turned out to be Harrison, Amelia Nell up and in it too, a white girl with less chance than a black boy of surviving a charging Leroy.

There it be, in a nutshell, my poor boy's life fate: too much to do, too many to help, and all to be done instant.

Still he tried, Lord, he tried. Managed to break most of Amelia Nell's first fall, fist in the eye and shirt ripped as thanks. Too close to catch that second shake-off, Amelia Nell flying higher, farther. Once

Harrison left ground he didn't need outside help, is the truth. The boy's an athlete, trained in courtside curl and roll.

"That girlfriend of yourn climbs me again, both of ya'll end up beside the nigger."

Giving orders, Leroy was, getting them too.

"I want that nigger outta here, I said. All the way out. Now."

Rest of those Mawatuck young'uns getting whiplash, trying to stare every direction at once: at the troll with missing fingers, at Amelia Nell flat on her back, at a balled up Harrison, at Lucian checking for damage, at the law arrived in the form of Donnie Anderson, at a nub count-off of charges The Lido's proprietor wanted filed: *disturbing the peace, breaking and entering, anything else you can think to charge the nigger with.*

It's agitation to this still night, it is, my Lucian's worrying. Soon as the past lets up, future starts its hectoring, pushing hard for answers. After he picks up that ribbon-tied diploma—then what? Try to till and plant and harvest this sorry wedge of land himself?

What's ahead is brighter than moonlight paints. Pretty soon Wayne's gonna offer to partner up, divide the profits. My boy won't end up the richest man in Mawatuck, but he'll earn enough to make his mama proud, pay taxes without a squabble. Would like to ease his mind on that point, but the dead don't have that privilege. Future and its profits will arrive when they do and Lucian's got to wait for that coming just like the rest of the living.

Ole stray tomcat slinks up to join the brooder, leans in for a rub. Stroking animal fur lifts the spirits no matter how low those spirits have sunk. Does the same for Lucian until something darker than shadow passes across my hanging tree.

A tease of mine, that hanging tree, never meant it to haunt.

After the government boys paid their first visit, Lucian still too young for school, he and I sitting at the breakfast table, him licking pancake syrup off his thumb.

"See that oak, son? Next to the chicken coop?"

Clear view of it through the kitchen window.

"Uh-huh. Harrison climbed to the top."

"All the way, Lucian?" Rosie interrupted, finishing up her own pancakes at the stove. "You sure about that?" Giving him chance to amend his fib.

"Uh-huh," Lucian said and I saw, though he couldn't, Rosie shake her head, grin.

"Tell you another thing that tree's good for, besides entertaining Harrison. All else fails, them government boys close in, your daddy can tie a noose to that lowest branch, hang himself."

"Clarence!"

Rosie's grin gone, Lucian's thumb stuck, me giggling.

"Quit talking nonsense. Your son will think you're serious."

"Set your mama straight, boy. Tell her you know the difference between sense and nonsense."

Leaned in closer, winked.

"I said enough, Clarence! You'll be causing nightmares."

Closer to vision than nightmare is what I caused.

That very evening Lucian climbed out of the bed his mamma had tucked him into, tiptoed over to the window to keep watch over my dark hanging tree. Now that I'm sharing his then, I feel his breath catch, chest heave from the image he sees, that I made him see: me lashed to the bottom limb, to-ing and fro-ing, rope cutting deep into my neck, but me still giggling, swinging and giggling, giggling and swinging.

Fearing a daddy dead's not the same as wanting him so, I don't care what's claimed otherwise. My boy didn't celebrate his daddy's corpse in vision or in life. But this night we're discussing—I ain't dead yet, not to the world, not to Lucian. I've just snuck out the back door. Lucian's almost coaxed that cat into his lap when I crank up the tractor and that fur ball goes clawing for cover.

I can't argue it was a good sign: me driving the Oliver while Mawatuck slept, riding in circles, cutting up the barnyard, giggling at night's pageant.

"Lucian! You'll hurt yourself!"

In motion by then, Rosie's son and mine, leaping for the metal that bridges wheel and seat, a platform dangerous narrow. But he makes it, lands where he needs to land to grab the ignition keys, me and Lucian and Oliver rolling on till we stop in front of Rosie in her nightgown.

"Time for bed, Dad."

Too old for Daddy all of a sudden?

Lord, don't it grieve.

My hands still on that Oliver's steering wheel, in charge of a machine going nowhere.

"Just taking myself a little spin."

"Take it tomorrow," Lucian says. "Tractor'll be waiting, same spot."

Tractor, maybe, but not the keys to run it.

"It's all right, Mama. Go back to bed. I'll see to Daddy."

"I tried to take the keys away," my Rosie says, sounding so weary why didn't I notice, first time around?

"He fought me for them. Wouldn't let go."

Did I?

I scarce remember.

"Don't worry about it, Mama. No harm done."

"The both of ya'll go in."

Must have wanted to keep planning my latest scheme.

I scarce remember.

But I remember my boy's return once he got his mama settled, taking up residence on the porch swing, smoking through a pack of cigarettes while I pursed my lips and puttered, imitating tractor as best my abilities would allow.

Mabel

"We're not finished with that hem, Missy. But until I see some chewing and swallowing going on, that needle and thread stay put."

Black and blue as the thunder and lightning storm the Lord refuses to sanction. Banged up elbows on the table. Thinking hard on something other than the breakfast set before her once steaming, now congealing. Makes me wince, those bones grinding formica, and mine aren't the nerves attached.

Shove that food plate a little closer, regardless.

Girl can brood and eat same time.

I do it, plenty.

Eventually a fork gets raised high enough to stir what don't need stirring.

Can't take too much of that messing. Didn't let the young'un mangle food as a toddler and not about to start when she's old enough to frequent a dancehall patrolled by men ought to be leashed themselves. But getting tossed around The Lido's not the issue just now. The issue is getting that graduation dress hemmed.

"Eat it or leave it be, Amelia Nell. You're not making mud cakes."

"Sorry," she says, a hushed sorry, eyes mighty glisteny as she inches that porcelain back where it started.

"Your grandma's sorry too. Sorry she's not taught you a body needs food to operate. Eating's not a choice, Amelia Nell, it's a necessity."

"I can't eat, Mabel. And even if I tried, it wouldn't stay down."

"Well now that's something else entirely. You feeling sick to your stomach?"

"Feeling sick of the world, if you must know."

Must know. I heard it.

"No eighteen-year-old's seen enough of the world to be sick of it."

"That's a crock."

And that's a fresh one. But while I'm trying to think up something fresher, she grabs hold of my dishwater slick hand, bumping a wounded elbow in the process.

"Sorry, sorry. I don't mean to take it out on you. It's just that...if we'd known in advance what Harrison was planning..."

"You'd have done what?"

"Lucian and I could have...I don't know. Worked together to trip Leroy."

"Trip Leroy? So he could have pitched you down the stairs after he flung you across the room? Tell me again how that helps Harrison Doxey?"

"I tell you how." Pinches up a piece of unbattered flesh on her wrist, shoves it at me. "To make sure THIS color ended up on the landing too."

"Two young'uns with broken necks are never better than one, whatever their shade."

"You don't understand."

"I understand that dress won't get hemmed by my wishing it. Baccalaureate's fast approaching. So let's get this job over and done with."

"I'm not going."

Reared back like a struck mule, I did.

"Say again."

"I'm not going."

"Because of a few bruises? Should have thought of that before you tackled Leroy."

"It's not about how I LOOK. It's...God! It's being cooped up in that Home Ec classroom beforehand, changing into a white robe, having all the other white robes swirling round me, squealing: 'Nell, Nell, tell us what REALLY happened.' And even if I refuse, Allison and Melinda will tell. 'Ya'll remember how Nell used to shimmy up the jungle gym in elementary school? Exactly like that she shimmied up Leroy.'"

"You ain't yet figured how to silence mouths like that?"

"And what if I do shut them up? Then what? March into that gym, acting like nothing's changed? Act like we're not 48 minus one, letting Mrs. Broome count off and shove me down plastic so I can waltz onstage and pick up a piece of paper? A lousy piece of rolled up paper?"

"Graduating high school's not about one night. It's about twelve years of passing tests and doing homework and earning the grades that get you to that night."

"I can't do it, Mabel. I can't sit on a folding chair and listen to people go on and on about the glorious future when Harrison's sitting in Mawatuck jail. I just can't."

Hardly finishes that quivering speech before she's out the door, crashing through wisteria tendrils, stirring up a hundred potent blooms, fragrances wasted on a troubled child. From the sink window, I see well enough where she's heading, to the deep back of the garden. But on a day still as this one, every window wide, she'd have to flee farther to keep her grandma from hearing sobs she means to defeat by holding breath.

Not working, that choke-back strategy. Never has.

Comes back all too clear, the sound of strangled sobbing when I thought she was safe in the trailer, playing jacks, or out by the shed, taming that wild rabbit she'd adopted. Instead I find her and her scrawny arm stretched out over a copperhead, far edge of the garden. Viper coiled up sunning but likely any second to wake and feel crowded. Amelia Nell struggling mightily to keep still, hold that arm straight, tears rolling down her cheeks.

"Watch yourself, young'un," I warned before the hoe sliced through tomato stalks to snake meat, some of that scatter landing on the young'un's thigh.

"Why you stretching that poor arm over a nasty viper anyway? Practicing to be a snake charmer?"

Wouldn't answer for clinging to me. Like I was the last solid object on this rotating earth.

"Tomato plants hid him?"

Half a nod.

"I was reaching for a ripe one and there he was—underneath."

He. That was the first time I had to cover a laugh.

"Uh-huh. So how long you figure that arm hung stranded?"

"REAL long," she said.

"Then aren't you the smart one?"

Pulled out of the hug, suspecting her ole grandma of making fun.

"Smartest trick I ever heard. Waiting out a copperhead. I knew I didn't raise no dummy."

Once she trusted the compliment, eager as a ferret to demonstrate her "smart" technique all over again for grandma's inspection.

"See? I had to hold it just like this. For an hour AT LEAST."

"Hour, is it?"

"At LEAST."

Tears, fright, pins and needles arm forgotten. Took off skipping toward the trailer for a peanut butter sandwich to "build up strength" in case "that snake has a buddy."

Rest of the day, past supper, past her bath, she embroidered her tale, a happy young'un reliving adventure. But something happened to change that mood once the lights went off. Conscience must have stepped out of those dark shadows, started haggling. *Your grandmamma hadn't come round with that hoe, you'd be a goner. You think you were brave? Think again, girlie. Lucky's what you were. Just plain lucky.* I'd just got settled in the rocker when out she traipsed, fingers in her mouth, gown tail in a knot.

"What's the matter, Missy? Feeling puny?"

Big toe digging hard at rug braids.

"You know how I said I held my arm stiff for three hours?"

"I believe three was the last number I heard out of your mouth."

"Okay, okay!" she said to nothing I could see beside her. "I'm getting to it."

"Who you talking to, young'un?"

"I'm TRYING to talk to you, if someone will LET me."

I let that pass. You can't expect a kid to explain everything.

"Having trouble falling asleep? That it?"

"I am," she said, a little bolder. "Because, well, I think maybe I was wrong about something."

Worrying that rag rug with a full set of toes by then.

"Uh-huh. What's that?"

"I think...I'm thinking maybe I didn't hold my arm over that snake for quite three hours."

"Not quite three, you don't think. Hard to judge time hanging over a snake, I imagine."

Teasing a little, but holding back the laugh.

"If you hadn't come, that snake would have gouged me for sure."

Couldn't keep a straight face after that. Cackle popped out of me like a firecracker and that cackle, coupled with the strain of confession, caused the young'un to burst into another round of tears. Had to take her into my lap, make room for two in that narrow rocker, forego backbone building for some serious coo and coddle.

Probably should have done more coddling all along the way, let that backbone business take care of itself. But I did what I did. No undoing it now.

"What's all this crying, Missy? You kept that arm safe until the hoe arrived, didn't you? Did your part, didn't you? Your grandma just happened by with a sharp blade."

Would have agreed to anything long as I let her sit in my lap—that much I realized. But the time's come now to show faith in her good sense with something beyond a shared seat. What she says, I can't dispute. Last night counted as a kind of graduation too, men rougher than Enon Halston in charge of the ceremony.

"Amelia Nell?"

No answer, but I know exactly where she is. Down by the trellis, alongside a stretch of peace roses.

Cane makes plenty of racket, dragging and scraping, but coming up on her sitting in dirt, jabbing her kneecap with a twig, I still cause a start. She's that far away in her head.

"Last time I saw this many bruises on you was after you'd leapt out of a wheelbarrow."

"I bruise easy. You always said that."

"But that time the bruising was your grandma's fault. The johnny-jump-ups needed weeding and you weren't quite walking yet, so I set you in a wheelbarrow next to me. Turned my back and you took a gainer into crabgrass."

"I probably cried then too."

"Squalled like a banshee."

"So I was...clumsy."

"Weren't entirely sure on your legs. But why would you be? Hardly spent any time upright."

"Couldn't have been hurt that bad if I squalled."

Blaming herself for the fall and the squall.

"When a young'un cries after tumbling two feet or ten, she ought to be comforted, not hushed. That was my first mistake: thinking if I made too much of the accident you'd never climb a tree or jump a ditch."

"Where's the mistake in that? Sounds logical to me."

"Well it wasn't. Your grandma was wrong. Like she's been wrong about a lot of things."

Peers at me peculiar because I'm sounding peculiar. Not our usual kind of chat, seasoned by tears or dry. But now that I've started, I've got to keep going. Say what needs to be said, do what needs to be done. Stop waiting for some exact right moment that might never come.

"You're kidding, right?"

"You see levity on this face?"

"Jesus, Mabel! I fell out of a wheelbarrow. It wasn't *your* fault."

"Plenty was my fault, but that's not what I drug myself out here to say. Those bruises on you now, the ones you got defending a friend, whether or not that defense was a lost cause, they're ample proof you didn't grow up a coward, no matter how many mistakes I made in the raising."

"Oh, yeah. I did Harrison a big service all right. Jumping Leroy. You weren't wrong about that either. You were exactly right. All I accomplished was pissing the goon off double."

"Maybe. But your friend was in a fix and you tried to help him."

"TRIED. What's that worth? Half a breath?"

"Whole Lido mess is another discussion entirely. Just now we need to return to that graduation topic. When you announced you were skipping the festivities, I should have said fine. Whatever the reason, your decision. You're not a kid in a wheelbarrow anymore. It's not my place to decide for you. You decide for yourself."

"I just can't bear to go, Mabel. I can't."

"I hear that. That's why I'm giving you your present right now. Come back inside with your grandmama. No need for either of us to wait any longer."

Harrison

It's like Mitchell Sears is trucking beside me through this nighttime jailhouse, whispering instructions in my ear. And me LISTENING, man, listening to that stoned white boy's tour notes in a place packed black.

Keep strolling, keep strolling. Give it some swagger, some ATTITUDE.

Welcoming committee lined up, knuckles showing. Nothing else skinny enough to slip through bars.

Expected bright, walking through dim. Like Mawatuck County wants to save on its electric bill.

"Lookee here."

"I'm lookin', I'm lookin'."

"What you figure, huh? Forgot to tell his mama he was stealing her car."

"That sounds 'bout right."

Lido in the rearview mirror, Donnie Anderson pulled over to the side of the road, took out his handcuffs key, used it. Didn't say: "There you go, bub," or "You're welcome." Didn't say squat, just turned around again, flipped the signal light and drove on.

Hands free, all the way here.

But not now, man. Cuffs back on for this stroll.

"This is it," announces Deputy Don.

Like I can't see or smell for myself.

Open pisser.

Mattress the odor of ripe feet.

Throw back your head. Laugh. LAUGH NOW, man!

Must have hit a wrong note in that laughing tune.

"Easy, son. Best get some sleep, if you can."

Except as soon I lay down, I start shaking head to toe, cot shaking with me.

In the backseat of that cop car, in cuffs or out: docile as dirt. Brain not firing a thought except: shit, shit, shit. Shit, shit, shit. Porch lights shining, up and down the beach road, up and down Mawatuck County, welcoming home somebody. Light shining on the Doxey's porch too. Joined by house lights soon as that telephone started ringing, call went through.

"You got a son named Harrison? Better come on down to the jailhouse then."

Should have told Lucian: "Warn Mama and Daddy."

Better Lucian than Mawatuck law.

Maybe better.

Mama in her bathrobe, Daddy, cross and sleepy, yelling: "Is this your idea of a JOKE, Lucian? Where's Harrison? Tell us!"

And Lucian not able to tell a thing more than he already had if I'd sent him to tell: Your son. Arrested. One hour ago and counting.

Most in here? Happy to see a deputy's back, be rid of a redneck, I'm guessing. But if I could keep Donnie Anderson in here with me—me, him, cuffs, pistol, cozied up together like cell pals—I'd snatch that chance like a loose rebound.

Because once he leaves, once he leaves, man, it's just me and them.

"Tell the truth. What cho in here for? Dealin' weed or something with a little more kick?"

"Cat got his tongue or he just busy pissing his pants?"

"He ain't gonna talk to us, Evan. Thinks he's too good for this joint. I can see that right now. One of those uppity blacks."

"You uppity too!"

"Hell yes. This jail's full of uppity blacks."

Mocking me, themselves, the world inside, out.

"Dealin' is what it is, got to be. Check out that swanky shirt, shoes too. Boy ain't poor."

"So what's your cut these days?"

Say: "The usual, man. The usual."

Was that Mitchell Sears's brag? Mountain-twang laying it on thick, trying to bullshit bullshitters. *"Biggest goddamn dealer this podunk county's ever caught, that's who."*

Audience thinking *biggest MILK-ASSED dealer, maybe. MAYBE.*

Out of his league, Mitchell Sears. Same as me.

"He don't feel like chattin', Sylvester. Don't want to 'so-ci-ate with our kind. Figures same money bought him that fine shirt and shoes gonna buy him out of a cellblock too."

Truth or con? Will cash get me out? Tonight?

"Look at him, pretending to snooze. Like we don't know the difference 'tween a man sleep and dead."

What the hell does that mean?

Soon as I bolt up, they laugh.

Laugh and laugh and laugh at nothing funny. Black boys die all the time in jails. Healthy black boys. Ask Jocelyn McPherson.

Congratulations, Harrison. Congratulations for parking your ass exactly where every honky wants it. Congratulations for proving every bigot in Mawatuck County right.

Shit, shit, shit.

That's my choice? Listening to Mitchell Sears or Jocelyn McPherson?

Shit.

Maybe no one will tell her.

Shit.

Probably heard already. Heard and fuming.

"Harrison Doxey?"

White voice asking—but not Donnie's.

"I'm Harrison."

"I'm Harrison—I'm Harrison—I'm Harrison" up and down and back again.

"Message from a friend of yours—someone named Lucian."

Reading off a slip of paper, like it's a book's worth of detail.

"Says to tell you not to worry about the Firebird. That he went back with Jimmy Barnard and got it. Wanted you to be sure to know he was the one drove it back to your house. Him and not Jimmy."

"Thanks."

"You hear that? Owns a Firebird. Fancy shoes and a Firebird. Sitting pretty, ain't he?"

"Was."

"One more thing," the deputy says. "This Lucian promises he'll come by tomorrow—if you're still here. Otherwise he'll see you back home."

"How come he's getting out, deputy? Who's he got working for him, we ain't?"

"Rest of ya'll settle down. Excitement's over for the night."

"Hear that? Ain't got no worries, this one. Friends and money rushing to his defense any minute."

Dressed in prison-visit clothes, carting cakes and flowers, paying me a visit just like the three of us paid Mitchell Sears.

Shit, shit, shit.

"Look at him, Evan. Ever seen anything like it? Brother scared white?"

Clarence

Night smells just like it should: deep and dank and mixed up with scent of pine and swamp. Rosie beside me, another combination of scents: Ivory soap and talcum, her own sweet Rosie self in there too. Beside me in our marriage bed, breathing like each breath's a joy and wonder, urging me with that rhythm to relax along with her, give in to sleep and dream.

But the fella she calls husband ain't interested in departing for dream just yet, enjoying too much the swamp music of crickets and bullfrogs, screech owls and whippoorwills, feeling snug and safe in lush darkness, free of Washington enemies still burning the midnight oil, working hard on new ways to make two and two add up to five. More than content, Clarence Carter, eyes wide in a room of shadows.

Sentimental, foolish, but a dead man's gonna wax nostalgic for the man he was every now and again. No help for it. Big, crazy, lazy Clarence with his fine shock of hair, scrubbed clean after his midnight tractor ride, sunk onto line-dried sheets, as much or more in love with the woman nestled alongside as when he was a courting man in Ocean Park.

Back and back and back again I go as Clarence the spook to hover over Clarence the man and my Rosie in our marriage bed before Wednesday dawns wispy as a feather, bringing what it brings to me and mine and all the rest: Cousin Mabel trying to force bacon fat down her grandchild's gullet, arguing over a dress hem, Amelia Nell digging in her heels, saying no, no, no, not going to that gym, to graduation, to none of it. Harrison Doxey, poor fella, pacing that closet-sized cell, prepping for a face to face with Jean and Furillo, upstanding citizens, conscientious parents, scarcely able to believe they're having to post bail for their upstanding, conscientious son. Donnie Anderson finagling to cut a deal with stump-fingered Boss, get the charges dropped, hardly breaking and entering, come now, no door or window busted through, nothing broken but the intruder himself. Donnie laying out the difference between getting the better of one retired military man, Virginian at that, and getting the better of the whole NAACP, suggesting Boss might want to pause and reconsider—Boss's choice, naturally. That girl always after Harrison to do what he ain't done doing some pacing of her own, back and forth in front of a bedroom wall covered with slogans and raised fists, forced to weigh the merits of what one black boy accomplished without her aid or knowledge. Clueless Enon, chugging coffee, no idea the wrench Mabel Stallings just tossed in his plans. My own Lucian and Rosie wondering how I ferreted out those well-hidden tractor keys and me, me, on that Oliver, bumping hard over clumps of dead brush and weeds until one stubborn cuss piece of tree just won't give, surprising both man and machine.

Mabel

"I'd planned on giving it to you after commencement, once I'd wrapped it pretty."

"Wait, then."

"Same gift, wrapped or unwrapped."

Dragging on my arm, bunching up close, fighting to keep me with her in that living room barely big enough for two when one was infant-size.

"You're going to have to let go of me so I can get it from under the bed."

"But you *planned* to wait. So you should. Wait."

Fear talking. No pleasure for me to see that fear, but I've got to believe it's not abiding.

"We've been through this twice already, Amelia Nell. You're as graduated as you'll ever be."

Ordinary shoebox, tied up with twine. Other people swear by bank vaults, lockboxes, but this piece of paper I wanted where I could reach out and touch it when the spirit moved.

Even without ribbons and bows it's official. County authorized and recorded.

"I'm ready, Mabel. I've got it back on. Looks pretty straight to me."

In that half-hemmed dress and on the table too, fierce pretending she's still got something to wear that outfit to.

Don't even slow in the pass-by. Rocker's where I'm bound.

"You want me to get the sewing basket?"

Chattering, chattering.

Chatter all she wants, she's going to open this box. Accept what's inside.

"Forget about that dress. Come sit beside your grandma. Here. On the footstool."

Climbs down off the table, gets that far, that close.

"Sit, I said."

When she does, bony knees jut past her chest. Where's evidence of the confidence ought to be her birthright? Got to be there, somewhere beneath that surface shimmy. Got to be. Because she's the only Stallings left, backbone or none.

Twice try handing her the shoebox, then set it on her lap.

"Open it. There ain't no copperhead in there. Nothing that bites."

Fingering it. Still fingering.

"Thank you."

"You don't know what you're thanking me for yet. Open the damn shoebox, Amelia Nell. You don't do it this second, I will."

"All right! All right!"

Confused her, that document, signed and stamped with the courthouse seal.

"I don't understand."

"Then read it through again."

"I understand what it SAYS, I just mean...it doesn't make sense. You're...here. Still here."

"And hope to be a good while yet. But that's no reason I can't sign the farm over to you."

"But the farm is yours!"

"Was mine. Now it's yours. Has been, officially, since March."

"But I don't know anything about running a farm!"

"You know more than you think. You've been watching your grandma run one for eighteen years."

"Like I pay attention to what you do."

Chattering to chatter again. Won't distract me that way. Not today.

"Your great granddaddy Caleb deeded it to me. Now I've deeded it to you. That's how family farms stay family farms. Passed down, generation to generation."

On the verge of using that ragged hem as a snot rag till I reach out, stay her hand.

"I can't accept it, Mabel."

"Why's that?"

A gamble. How do I know she won't answer something I can't bear to hear?

"I just can't. That's all."

"Don't think you can stand up to Enon, is that it?"

"What's Enon got to do with this?"

"Such a fast reader you missed the fine print. No sale to Halstons, current or future. Leave it to the buzzards or moccasins, deed it to Goodwill, but no Halston gets it at any price. That's my one condition, pure and simple. Got no answer the first time, so I'm asking again. Can you stand up to Enon?"

"Of course I can stand up to Enon!"

"Mack, too? No soft spot for the vulture's son?"

That got a snotty sneer.

"All right then. It's settled. If you can fend off Halstons, you can choose corn seed and rule Luther."

Heart thumping hard enough to hurt before I finish that mouthful.

But I've said what I intended. Rest of the persuasion has to come from what's outside this trailer. Woods and fields and hedgerows. Green growth and gray dirt. Land that's been her familiar since she could crawl.

"This is really what you want? Me taking over? Already?"

"It is."

"So, starting today, I'm the one supposed to make Enon's life a misery?"

"That's the idea. Think you can handle it?"

"The making Enon's life a misery part? Fuck yeah," she says, those scabby legs and bruised arms and puffy eyes never lovelier to her old grandma.

Harrison

Mitchell Sears is SUCH a fucking liar, man.

Jail night is endless. Endless.

Time's passing. That much you know because the snores on either side get louder, softer, gulped, know by the clink clink clink of somebody else's restless sleeplessness, up and roaming a closed circuit. Otherwise no first timer knows jack about what to do/not to in Mawatuck Prison, Mitchell Sears included. Swagger, useless. Humility, worse. White, brown or otherwise, no fresh meat's gonna crack the code.

Un-a.

Except, turns out, what hits you, what you realize in a flash?

Realize and shudder from?

Only rule that matters?

Here till you ain't, man.

Here till you're out.

And when they get here? Jean and Furillo? Looking tense, feeling betrayed? What's my excuse? What am I supposed to say? Confess to selfishness? Admit it wasn't for the "cause" or "our people," just fucking for me? Just my lonesome self wanting inside Boss's Lido to drink beer with Nell and Lucian?

Check Mama's hands—gotta remember. Do that right away. See if she's carrying a handkerchief, see if it's already wadded. Check if Daddy walks in frowning normal or frowning like he's being gouged by straight pins.

Get my sorrys out all at once.

Don't ask why they didn't show up sooner, get me out quicker, because maybe they did try. Tried and tried and tried but no lawyer would pick up the telephone past midnight, NAACP counsel included.

Get ready, man. Get prepared for the lecture. Harrison Doxey, disappointing fuck-up. Son who let down his parents. Black who let down his RACE.

"This is them, I betcha. Mama and Daddy coming with the cash now."

And it is—but not only them.

Shit.

Shit, shit, shit.

Roaring at me, fire in her eyes, and no escape, man.

No fucking escape.

"Harrison Doxey! Harrison Doxey!"

Squalling my name, Jocelyn McPherson, but...wait.

Not like she's mad, more like she's desperate. Desperate to get to me, snatching at me through metal bars like I'm candy-covered Christmas, like I'm some kind a prize she's being denied.

And why is that?

Why is that?

"Look-a-there, Enon. Got himself 'nother kind of fine stash. Boy's got all the luck, ain't he? Hey, mama. Hey, papa. Hey, girl."

Mama and Daddy, drawing up, drawing in, like that prison-house razz is akin to typhoid, but Jocelyn McPherson, ignoring everything and everybody but me, man, laughing, clapping, grabbing, saying what I can't believe she's saying but she is saying it. She *is*.

"Harrison Doxey! NEVER have I been so proud!"

Clarence

Interested in a man's last thoughts? What he sees and thinks, end upon him? What a pine grove resembles on last observance? What air smells like in short supply? The message a doomed man hears in birdsong sung especially for him?

Even if I confide, you won't strain to remember. No reason for interest till you're in the same position and then, well, you've got your own tale to tell about slow rot or sudden takeout, whichever your fate.

Me, I'm not a bit sorry I finished in the Oliver's company. Tractor and me went way back, spent some of my happiest hours occupying that wide-bottomed seat. A secondhand piece of farm equipment when I bought it, installment plan, but Lucian greased and tuned it, got it running smooth as a tractor can in its middle age and mine. Probably started out fire engine red but sun and dust and wind burnished that bright to autumn hue, the color of maple leaves falling.

See how a mind fixed on decline starts seeing finale in every little detail?

But listen: that Wednesday morning, my hand was on the steering wheel, not in a tight clinch maybe but holding on good enough to navigate, so what you've heard on that score's wrong too: Clarence Carter wasn't driving with his knees. I *was* sniffing dust, kicked up from tractor wheels. I was headed for a curtain of pine, the only shade to be found on a cut of land already burning with sunshine and not even eight o'clock. I did feel an itch backside of my knee, scratch at it through my overall pants, and while I was digging chanced to notice cow manure on the foot clutch, courtesy of my brogans, and tried to knock it off before the front wheel smacked stump.

That half of half a second when I might have braked or swerved or otherwise kept that tractor wheel from mounting dead oak? Come and gone, my friend, come and gone. The Lord's will and a mortal's absent-mindedness flipped big ole Clarence through air like a weightless slip of a thing and heading toward bone crush and blood burst I accepted both with a grin and giggle because Clarence the man had had his life run and ride, see, and now that part was over.

Clarence

Clarence Carter, coffin-wedged and -stuffed, but up and out and circling too, flying high and wide, taking in the Mawatuck sights, a dead man all a sudden in the deep-down know about what was and will be.

Round-up time, folks.

Time for this spook to spread some relief and cheer, some disappointment too.

Reverend Clevon Dunston of New Providence Baptist is still last-minute practicing his baccalaureate address, aiming for perfection on behalf of the Lord and the mixed community. Standing in front of cracked latticework and limp palms, the Reverend's planning to caution the Class of '68 about troubled waters ahead, warn young'uns like Culdy's boy, Jimmy, he'd best invest in swimming lessons, though the Barnard slouched on folding chair won't be listening, transistor radio plug in his ear. Regardless of who will or won't pay heed to the Reverend's message, best way to prepare for the occasion, get himself in preacher fighting form is, right now, shut off the air conditioning in his den and practice in swelter. 'Cause in Mawatuck gym it's gonna be as close and stuffy as it is in Zion Baptist, funeral hour.

Strange it is to peer down into your own coffin, get a distant view of head hair tamed by a mortician but still looking mighty full and fine.

Inspired by Elmer Dockery's backyard pile of flat tires and scrap iron, I used to tell Rosie: "My time comes, sling me out with the egg shells. Our trash heap's far enough from the house. You won't smell me sour."

And Rosie would roll her eyes, say: "Lord a-mercy. Me outlast you? Clarence Carter will put ten wives in the grave before he passes."

Ah my Rosie. She's a beauty in black, even though it grieves me to see her dressed in Lily Arnold's favorite color. Looking a little too peaked, but shoulders back, chin up, facing forward while Lucian's squirming round like a five-year-old, trying to spot friends he don't yet see.

Show up for Daddy's funeral. Just show up. That's not a hell of a lot to ask, is it?

"Patience, son," I whisper. "They'll get here."

Not easy, though, picking out particular folks in a church this crammed, pews overloaded despite temperatures in mock of hell. The curious, that's mostly who's here. Not that many in Mawatuck realize they're going to miss ole Clarence, not that many truly sorry to see me go so soon after the fact of the going.

But Sis, she's in a state. Has been since she got word of my demise. In a state and, same time, being a nuisance. Up at the house, Wednesday afternoon, urging Rosie: "Go ahead, honey. Cry."

Rosie slumped in a living room chair, kneading a work shirt of mine she'd been rinsing when told she was a widow. Every time Lucian tried to take that damp bundle from his mama, Rosie clamped down tighter.

"Let it out, honey," Irene pestered. "It's no good holding in what needs release."

"Leave Mama alone."

"Leave her alone, Lucian? When your mama's in shock, grieving just like me, Clarence's only sister? I'm telling you and your mama too: it's best to give in. Just give in and let the tears slide."

Might be best for folks like Irene. But Sis hardly qualifies as your standard.

Kitchen already filled up with cakes and hams and casseroles, whole fried chickens and fried chicken parts. Soups and roasts, green beans and pecks of early tomatoes, stewed corn and mustard greens, cornbread, spoon bread, potato salad, chicken salad, plus a fine looking strawberry shortcake I was hoping somebody would sample, but nobody did. Tomcat, at least, didn't let that bounty go to waste. Leapt onto the counter every chance he got to paw and gnaw another chicken liver.

Through with urging tears, Irene moved on to a fresh list of oughts.

"There's thank you notes to write and a notice for the church bulletin. And we've got to decide soon what kind of service we want. You can't just let a preacher say whatever comes into his head."

But come the occasion he does: calling my corpse a good Baptist when its only claim to the faith was a river dip as squalling infant. Works in a tribute to my government defiance too—a preacher, but born Southern.

"In the meantime, you've got to keep up your strength, Rose. There's a table full of food in there. Not a bit of it will last in this heat."

"Take what food you want, Irene."

"And have people say I was carting off food brought for you and your mama? Even though a *sister's* surely entitled."

"Take it! Mama needs to rest."

"We all need to rest, but we can't right now. Your mama's got to decide what she's going to wear to the funeral. Whether we're going to bury your daddy in the family plot or Mawatuck Cemetery. And that's just the beginning. Rose, honey, I'm sorry, just as sorry as I can be, but funerals don't plan themselves."

Lucian got a good grip on a freckle patch then and yanked it with him to the food room.

"Leave or shut your fucking mouth."

Irene, twisting out of that grip, had a comeback. Sure she did.

"And let your mama stay in that chair, squeezing on your daddy's shirt? You think that's a better idea, Lucian Leviticus?"

Wasn't so much thinking, my boy, as sorely wishing he'd locked the doors against Irene and all of Mawatuck's cakes and sweetmeats, shut down the funeral carnival before it got started. And if that made folks squawk and shake their heads, label the son crazy as his dead daddy, so what? Let the ghouls talk. Better Clarence crazy than Irene crazy.

Down at the Grill, Thursday, Wayne and Donnie Anderson both enjoying their morning shakes and fries before Mack Halston strolled in, convinced he had news to share.

"Word is Clarence Carter fought a tractor and lost."

"Something like that," said Donnie.

"Stupid cuss," said Mack.

"Not near as stupid as you!" Wayne sputtered, ashamed of himself because there he was, at the Grill, filling his stomach, stead of paying his respects up at the house, offering Lucian help and comfort.

"Mawatuck without the nut. It'll make your life easier, won't it, deputy?"

"Don't you and that mayonnaise burger have some place else to be?"

Good deputy can plot a "situation" developing three acts shy.

"Me? Naw," Mack said, buckteeth gummed with burger mush.

Buckteeth was what Wayne was aiming for, but since he missed, Mack held advantage before Deputy Don jumped in.

Funny, ain't it? Fists flying on account of Clarence Carter and not even family fists. That's gotta rate as some kind of accomplishment, don't it?

Hotheads brawling one end of Mawatuck, Rosie on the other, choosing a ground box, Alfred at her side with his checkbook and not pushing for cheap stuffing either. But once a body gets shoved in a spare-no-expense or otherwise coffin, that body and casket require accompaniment. In the viewing room. In the hearse. A no-exceptions policy that, come funeral day, stranded one of the living: Cousin Mabel's grandyoung'un left without a ride to Zion Baptist.

Decides to hoof it, Amelia Nell does, dressed in graduation shoes and dress. Look at that young'un. If she ain't Cousin Mabel's kin in every pore. Jaw set, eyes a-squint, kicking through grit to honor the dust we all become, not a God's breath chance in hell those white shoes will reach their destination looking anything but putty-colored. Cousin Mabel's dirt lane's got woods and swamp to shade it, but once Amelia Nell hits Bull Run, she's got another mile of glinting blacktop to trek, and so far none of that journey's helped her figure out why people automatically feel sorry for a memory-less orphan like herself but won't feel half as bad for Lucian saddled with eighteen years of knowing who he'll miss.

Just ahead, that mean little shack Enon Halston threw up for his laborer Horace Brooks and Ophelia, Horace's arthritis-suffering wife. Chimney lists, tar paper peeling from the plywood, the kind of tenant house makes the Carter place look half a mansion. But it's a palace to the rheumy-eyed mangy hounddog that bares what's left of yellow teeth at Amelia Nell Stallings.

"Who you pretending to hurt?" Ophelia quizzes, twisting round as best she can to see for herself.

"Hey, Ophelia."

"Hey, girl. Where you off to so dressed up? Too hot for walking."

"It is, but I've got to get to the church."

"Afternoon services at Zion Baptist? When ya'll start that?"

"Not regular preaching. A funeral. Clarence Carter's."

"Oh, uh-huh, I remember now, this was the day. One big white man, that Clarence Carter."

While Ophelia talks, Amelia Nell dumps dirt and pebbles from one shoe, then the other, loitering, lingering on purpose now, hoping that bent form will keep on talking, hound keep on snarling.

But Ophelia's got work to do. She can't be wasting too much time entertaining a skinny white girl with dirty feet.

"You take care then," she says, flapping her palm, turning away, but long after Ophelia Brooks makes her crippled way to the backyard, long after that watchdog loses interest in the harmless specimen other side of his narrow domain, Amelia Nell stays put, pretending she's on a rest break.

Since I'm dead I can go ahead, expose her true fear and be done with it. The girl's heading to my funeral for Lucian's sake, but every bit of her wants to avoid close-up, close-in contradiction of what she so fiercely wants to believe: that somehow her tough old crow grandma's gonna escape a mortal's fate, live forever, that final disappearance Cousin Mabel's been predicting these last fifteen years a fairy tale that won't come true, won't leave Amelia Nell with an absence that'll feel like her own little death, a sudden hole in existence because her grandma is somebody she does love, not just someone she's supposed to. Someone she can't bear to part with.

Thinks so, anyway. Before she can and does bear it.

About the time Amelia Nell's pushing her grubby feet back into grubbier shoes, Mabel's off to her garden, gearing up to tackle weeds that dared showed their stems overnight. Wearing her sunhat as well as gardening gloves, hauling along that walking cane too. But before you jump to the wrong conclusion: Cousin Mabel ain't snubbing Rosie. She plans to visit once the rest of Mawatuck has moved on to other sensations, visit the widow when the widow might enjoy some company, not while company's a chore to endure. Me, Cousin Mabel figures I'm body dead, soul free, happier than she is, still stuck in this aggravating world and wouldn't care besides who showed up at my funeral service.

Sharp as a tack about some things, Cousin Mabel. I never claimed opposite.

Deputy Anderson throwing Mack Halston out of the Grill on Thursday meant Enon's boy finished his mayonnaise burger in his daddy's truck, strewing bun crumbs on the seat, few on the dashboard too. So let's just say Enon's had Mack messes to contend with all week, blood pressure already on the climb before he starts out alone toward Mabel Stallings's farm and trailer. And you and I both know he's fixing to discover, this Sunday excursion, nothing to settle his nerves, years of strategy made worthless by a reassigned deed. In just a few minutes Enon's set to realize he's gotta start all over again, start from scratch, trying to tease farmland from the grip of a Stallings young as eighteen.

Meanwhile that new landowner's put on a burst of speed, clock ticking, hurrying past ditch banks thick with Queen Anne's lace, Edna Dowdy's crepe myrtle grove, Wayne's shut-down garage, air hose, spare parts, wrenches, dragged from sight, meter on the gas pump stuck between a four- and five-dollar sale, owner himself mashed up alongside the rest in that hot, hot church, dressed in a scratchy winter suit, losing business for Lucian's sake. Mechanic shop in Mawatuck's a seven-day-a-week venture. That's the schedule farmers expect and depend on and the reason Wayne needs himself a partner. But just now what's occupying Wayne is the grease and grime Borax left behind, bent so low to the task Lucian has to crane round twice more to spot wool amidst seersucker. But he does finally spot that material, he does.

Tell you what: my corpse's resting a lot more comfortable than a certain slice of Mawatuck citizenry, Sunday just past two. Men in choking ties, women in girding girdles, all of them packed tighter than canned fish, some of them starting to smell about as high. Pale faces pinking up despite those flapping church fans, cardboard Jesuses on a stick working overtime. Gent after gent excuses his way to the nearest window, convinced those swelled frames just need a stronger heft to let in another inch of blessed air.

Folks and their everlasting hope. Right funny to a corpse.

Heat's a misery, no question about that, but there's something else causing discomfort, anxiety of a more personal kind among those pews, a guessing game in progress of who alive and well in Zion Baptist today will next be coffin-bound.

Bertha Ambrose, fingering the bow at her wrinkled throat? Harvey Dowdy, jabbed awake by his wife's sharp elbow? Cousin Leonard, praying hard for forgiveness from the Lord for cheating the dead out of a horseshoe nickel? Irene? Powdered to the hairline white, floral handkerchief flapping around lips purple-red and active: "Oh Clarence, Oh Clarence, we'll miss you so..."

Can't pick your mourners—but you're supposed to be able to pick your friends.

Lucian again, 'cause he's seen Wayne but not Amelia Nell, finally close enough to Zion Baptist to hear the hymn Irene selected for openers.

Just as I am, without one plea.

Can a corpse sing along?

Tempted to try.

Harrison thinks he's hid that blue Firebird sufficient behind a paler blue hedge of hydrangea, but Amelia Nell spies those hubcaps no trouble at all.

"Hey."

When Harrison jumps so do the foam dice dangling from the Firebird's rearview mirror.

"Nell—Jesus."

"No. Just Nell."

Joker laughs, other won't.

Dressed in a suit to car sit at my funeral. You think that simple act of respect don't touch a dead man, you'd be wrong.

"Glad to see you..."

"Out of jail, you mean? Freed?"

Much as I like the boy, he's gonna have to get past touchiness on that point. It's part of his history now, part of who he is and will be.

"Well, yeah, out of jail, but I meant glad you came. To the funeral. Lucian will be too."

"Hymn's over."

Which it is. Hymn books and fans and fannies resettling.

"Hear me? Hymn's done."

Whether she does or doesn't hear, Amelia Nell keeps her own fanny planted against the Firebird, emptying gritty shoes again.

"Better hurry, no joke," Harrison says, nerves starting to squeak up his voice. "That preacher's set to drone."

"Come with me."

Slaps dashboard twice in such a good imitation of mirth his silver ID bracelet jangles in time with foam dice.

"I'm serious, Harrison. This is ridiculous, you listening from your car."

"Best seat in the house, girl. Right here."

"But Lucian would WANT you inside. He WOULD!"

"Tell him you saw me. That's enough."

"We'll just walk in together. Nobody will say anything."

Wrong there. People'd say anything and a lot more besides, but none of that matters to Cousin Mabel's grandyoung'un. She's convinced Harrison Doxey ought to be inside Zion Baptist and that's where she aims to drag him. Quicker than you'd expect, she snatches open the driver-side door, latches onto the boy inside and starts pulling. When Harrison pulls back, in she falls, tumbling headfirst into his lap.

"Jesus Christ!" he shrieks, scrambling out from under her. "You trying to get us both shot?"

"Okay, okay, sorry." Standing again, straightening her hem. "But I wish you would come in with me."

"Dive twice one week into a sea of white? Un-a."

Only reason Amelia Nell gives up soon as she does is the fear Lucian will think she stayed home too.

"I'll tell him then. That you came."

Crosses macadam, gets to within, oh, say a foot of the vestibule door when she feels the presence of company, turns and there he is: nervous as a squirrel, looking like he's on the way to Armageddon, but signed up regardless, entering one step behind before she grabs his hand to even them up.

I believe they feel the spark, both of them, on their own, but just in case they don't, I break the spook rule, add some extra jolt to that flesh connection. Harrison Doxey's a better fit for Amelia Nell Stallings than the superintendent's son and he ain't a boy will desert her either, once pledged. For a girl more afraid of desertion than rabies, what's better? It's true, hitched up with a girl like Jocelyn McPherson, Harrison would work harder on his people's behalf, but Cousin Mabel's granddaughter is the girl better able to comfort a man be he black or white. And soon as she gets over wanting the whole black race to love her, settles to the satisfaction of the love of one fine black-race boy, they'll be a good match. Better than good.

But just so that eventuality don't get thrown off by busybodies gasping first time they appear together in public, I give the preacher a little shove in the prayer direction and kill two birds, one stone. Blind the busybodies and clear a sight light for Lucian to see entering who he wants to see.

Prayer for the dearly departed in the Lord's hothouse, brethren, a prayer prayed over my big head and rouged cheeks and stitched together chest.

"Our heavenly Fatha, we come today over the earthly remains of your servant, Clarence Augustus Carter..."

Last chance for me to make the circuit, whisper in my Rosie's ear that she was the wife of wives, no one finer, no one I would have switched her for, no one else I ever wanted after catching the first glimpse of Rosalee Arnold, whisper to my boy that his dead daddy's peacock proud of how he's been sticking up for his mama, forbearing as best anyone could his Aunt Irene, telling him now what I should have told sooner: *Don't be afraid of a corpse, son, your daddy's or your own* because it's true what Cousin Mabel rants, people afraid of dying are afraid of living, useless to themselves and everyone around.

Back on that last row, scrunched over to the side—I see those two federal fellas, sure I do. Saw them soon as they started their side door sneak-in, trying to stay low profile. Should have figured they'd show up to double-check on the big man in the casket, make sure crazy Clarence truly was folded up in there and not some funning substitute. But you know what surprises this dead man? How relieved they look, dog-tired relieved. Sick of the Clarence Carter case, turns out. Sick of angling for what they were never going to get. Those early balding boys free of me and me of them.

Lord a-mercy, as Rosie would say.

That sonic boom wail? Came out of Sis's throat, throat and the rest of her making fast tracks for me, set to upset my carrying case, muss my final hairdo with a frantic goodbye squeeze.

Preacher's the first one tries to separate live flesh from dead but he's no match for Irene in flailing mode, so it falls to Lucian to pry his aunt's fingers from his daddy's neck, sling her on his hip and duck-step carry her back to the pew.

Watching that rough handling, Amelia Nell again reaches for Harrison Doxey. Watching that spectacle, Cousin Leonard remembers how Irene, as a little girl, used to squat to pee in the middle of a plowed field, not an inch of brush for cover. Watching that strangeness, two government boys bewildered by the antics of God-fearing, churched-in Crackers. Watching that nonsense, and I thank the Lord Almighty for it, Rosie dips her head to cover a smile that will break into a laugh soon as she and Lucian are back home alone, sitting at that laden kitchen table, sharing strawberry shortcake, putting aside their forks to snort like a mama and son do, when tickled, when blessed.

Got to speed up here, near to overrunning my allotment, so speed with me.

Enon's left Mabel's, but he ain't left her spitting and fuming, not this visit. He's left her cackling, twirling her walking stick like it's a fairy wand, poof and Enon disappears in a cloud of dust, poof and Enon gets his, cackling, twirling, when all of a sudden what was bright light speckles up and Cousin Mabel crumbles.

But wait now, don't start grieving on Cousin Mabel's account. It ain't her time yet; she's not finished with living. That faint was a scare, another one, but no coffin's being ordered up for that tough, wide body, no shortcake or other kind of sweet being cooked for delivery to that house trailer. Long before Amelia Nell returns, Cousin Mabel's recovered her color, feet propped on a footstool, electric fan blowing in her face. Able to hear, avid to hear, all about Amelia Nell's roadside adventure. Something for those two to share and snort over.

Goes something like this.

After the service, Amelia Nell gets plenty of ride-home offers—from Harrison, from Donnie Anderson, from Wayne, from Lucian too, but decides on walking nevertheless. Walking will give her

chance to think. And she's all of a sudden got some serious thinking to
do—none of it about the dead and earth-departed.

Sun's just as bright, day's just as hot, but the heat and dust and
dandelion fuzz of Mawatuck is no competition for heart storm. When
Enon and his truck pass first time, young'un doesn't even look up.

But you can bet Enon recognizes that scrawny landowner on the
stroll and sets that Chevy engine in reverse.

Picture it: Amelia Nell still walking, Enon in his truck slow-poking
backwards to keep up, travelling alongside. Enon's webby face pushed
out that open truck window, doing its level best to come off awfully
pleased by Amelia Nell's early inheritance.

Got to feel a LITTLE sorry for the man, don't you? In the position
he finds himself, no warning whatsoever? Come now. Down at the
bottom of that human kindness pocket? You do, don't cha? Little bit?

"Just heard the news, Amelia Nell. Your grandma says I'm supposed
to do my begging to you, now on."

"Is that what Mabel says?"

Still walking, still looking elsewhere, not a half glance at that
stretched-wide smile until Enon errs by saying aloud: "Hard to believe
Miz Mabel would go and do a thing like that, leaving a farm to a
young'un, but she says that's what she did."

Walker stops. Truck stops. Amelia Nell squints hard into that cab,
wondering how a man with Enon's bucks could be so feeble-minded.

"Do you imagine that's helping your case, acting like Mabel made a
mistake? Calling me a young'un to my face?"

"Aw, now, Miss Nell," Enon gushes quick. "I didn't mean to give
offense. Fact is, lot of people would be tickled to be called young'un.
Myself, for one."

"Uh-huh," says Amelia Nell.

Snaps a bit of lace weed from the ditch bank, whirls round, and
with that stem taps Enon's arm twice.

"So? I'm listening. What's your offer?"

A foot gets excited, same as the rest of a fella. Surge of gas and the pickup shoots backward, far enough that Enon elects to shout.

"You saying you're interested?'

"I'm saying name a price."

"I'd have to do some figuring."

"Better figure fast, Enon. Who knows how long I'll be inclined to take bids?"

Here's the part don't get shared with Cousin Mabel, no need it should. While Amelia Nell has Enon frying on that hot plate, she's doing some speculating too. If the farm IS truly hers, she COULD decide to rent to Enon instead of Luther Douglas, and with the profits build Mabel a real house, a replica of the one that burned. If she rented at a high enough price per acre, she could contribute to Harrison Doxey's lawyer fees, Rosie and Lucian's upkeep. With Halston money she could help out a lot of people, spread around the good fortune.

With Halston money.

If she took it.

"Say again?" Enon pleads, just about back beside her, taking care to light touch that gas pedal, tap it with his toe.

"I said you're testing my patience. What's the Stallings farm worth to you, acre by acre?"

Here's the thing about a Mawatuckian. Talk sharp and direct to them, they're compelled to talk the same, even after a lifetime's training in backtrack and meander.

The price Enon sputters is more than Luther Douglas or anyone else in Mawatuck and the three counties joining would or could pay for an acre of farmland subject to drought and flood, wind, raccoons and boll weevils.

Shame Cousin Mabel's not around in the flesh to witness the grand rebuke—no doctor could have fed her better medicine. Charmed my dead bones too, watching her childrearing efforts pay off so handsome, granddaughter waving off Mawatuck's richest tempter like he was a bothersome gnat.

"Wastin' precious breath, Enon," Amelia Nell declares, already planning how she'll stretch and embroider this moment, retelling the story to Mabel.

"Wastin' your breath and mine."

That rain Mawatuck farmers been so long waiting and praying for? Water desperate needed? It's a ways off yet, week or more, much as three, but it's coming to Stallings fields, Halston fields too, a drenching that'll start with thunder squall, heat lightning turned real, a pelting, heavy downpour offering drink to withered crops and flyaway dirt, muddying the earth atop the coffin of Clarence Carter, body deceased but spirit still laboring like a mule, like the devil himself, toiling hard and constant and far from through, friend, far far from through.